BOY FUN

A COLLECTION OF
TWENTY EROTIC STORIES

EDITED BY

LUCAS STEELE

Published by Accent Press Ltd – 2010
ISBN 9781907016097

Printed and bound in the UK

Cover design by
Adam Walker

Contents

Sand and Steel
by Shanna Germain

The man sucking me off knows what he's doing. He runs the flat of his tongue around the end of my dick before he suctions me into his mouth, bit by bit. His lips look pink and raw against the fabric of the black ski mask he wears. His eyes are bound over the mask, so his lips are all I see of his face. His lips sliding over me, taking me in. It takes all of my focus to keep from closing my eyes as he sucks me, and I know that this is what he wants. He wants me off my game, vulnerable to the suck and slither of his tongue and lips.

And I want him to think that he's so good at what he's doing that I have dropped my guard. So when he lets my dick slide from his mouth and leans down to tongue my balls, I decrease the pressure of the knife point against his neck. I moan to show him how he's getting to me, how I might let him live if he gets me off well enough. The moan is an act, but it's also part real. And that's the thing that's got my pulse thumping in my forehead. Even with his hands bound behind his back, he's a risk. And that, as much as his mouth, is why I'm so fucking hard.

He stops lapping my balls and puts his lips around the end of my dick again. I should stop him now, but I want just another minute inside the warm depths of his mouth. I want to face-fuck him just a bit longer. I already know he's not going to give up the information. He's too good. So I'm going to have to kill him. But first, I *want*. Fuck, I *want*.

I put my hands on each side of his black hood and pull his head toward me. He leans willingly, swallowing me up until my brain feels like it's whirl-pooling down into my stomach. His rhythm is hard and unyielding, a rough in and out that draws my balls up and my breath down.

'Ah, fuck.' I grab the back of his head and pull him off of me before I can come. It's harder than I expect. To buy a little breathing time, I hold his head away and say, 'I do love those pretty little lips of yours, especially against that black fabric. Like they're just made for sucking cock.'

My hard-on throbs in the air between us. He can't see it, of course, not with his eyes bound. It lessens some of his humiliation, but I can't risk having him see me. Not that he's going to get out of this alive, but I've been taught to cover all my risks.

I put my fingertip to his bottom lip. It's wet with his saliva and my pre-come. There's something about the way he sucks his lip in, under his top teeth, that reminds me of someone I used to know, a lifetime ago, but I can't place it.

'Now, I hate to waste a mouth like that. So let's call a truce. You give me what I want –'

I tap my palm against the side of his covered cheek to show I'm serious. 'And I'll think about letting you go.' It's a fair promise. As fair as I can make anyway.

He doesn't move or speak. He's hardly moved or spoken in the last five hours, which is why I resorted to having him suck me. I know what he's trained for: he can be buried alive; he can survive drowning and cold and heat. He can take pain. But pleasure? He's not trained for pleasure.

2

People on the outside think we're cruel and somehow inhuman. And we are; just not in the way they think. It's all about breaking our foes down, using fear and humiliation to protect what matters most.

But this guy doesn't seem to have either humiliation or fear. My men waited for five days for him to show and still they nearly missed him. Unlike a lot of guys nowadays, he actually knows how to do what needs to be done. I can tell from the way they bound his eyes without taking off his mask and from the ropes around his hands and feet that he put up a fight before I got here. I'm almost sorry I missed it. But there's something kind about having him be anonymous; when you do things like I do, it's easier if I never see their face.

And now we're alone, him and I, in this small concrete room in the middle of nowhere. Now we're alone with each other and our wills.

'C'mon,' I say. I bounce my hard-on off his lower lip, just to remind him why we're here. My dick reacts with its own little half-surge. I'm tempted to stick it back between those lips, to fuck his mouth until I come, but it's a temptation that I can't risk. Not yet. 'Tell me what I want to know.'

He says something, low enough that I can't hear. It's an old trick, and I'm not falling for it. You can stick your dick in a guy's mouth and he's smart enough not to bite it off, but you lean your face down there, and you don't know what could happen.

'Try again,' I say.

He licks his lips. The point of his tongue is wet with saliva and it leaves a trail across his top lip.

'Let me watch you come,' he says. 'I'll tell you what you want to know.' It's the first time I've heard his voice. Something about the deep spit of it sends a surge of blood into my dick, rising it a half-inch higher.

Without waiting for my answer, he searches for my dick, finds the end of it with his lips and sucks me inside. He moans and my brain shuts down in the warm wet suck.

'I don't believe you, you know,' I say, even as I'm reaching behind his head to take off the blindfold. My fingers shake, but the knot's not hard to undo. He sucks my dick in deeper, until I swear I can feel his lips against my stomach. I like to close my eyes when I come – it takes me into a space I can't capture otherwise – but I don't dare.

I pull the blindfold away as he bobs up and down on my dick, sucking it as though he's sucking up oil or gold. I drop the blindfold to the ground. And then, everything happens at once: I start to come inside the hot wet hole of his mouth, the man raises his blue eyes to my face, and I understand that I have fucked up.

I back up, sliding my twitching dick from his lips. Come sprays the air between us, but I barely notice.

'Jesus,' I breathe. 'Fuck, Jonas? What the fuck?'

The man's eyes flick toward me when I say his name. And then his lips curl up at the corners. 'Shit,' he says. 'No wonder you felt so good in my mouth. I should have known it was you.'

He says my name, and it's the same way he said it then. The same way he said it in that sugar cookie summer.

Sugar cookie summer. That's how we thought of it then, but that's not how I think of it now. Now, I think of it as Indoc summer. As the summer of sand and surf, of hypothermia and drown-proofing. As the summer we started out as boys and ended as men. The summer I almost rang Mother Moy's Black Bell. The summer of me and Jonas.

From day one of Indoc training, Jonas wasn't hard to spot. He was the only white boy in our class. Which isn't to say there weren't other white boys, but no one was as white as him, with his pale-pale skin and his beyond-blond crew cut. Even his eyes were as white as you could get and still have any colour in them. Blue, but like snow goes blue in the twilight. Only thing dark about him was his tattoo, a huge solid black dragon that lounged across his upper back and blew black smoke around his arm.

It was that arm I had a hold of as we waded into the seven-foot breakers, my feet turning to instant ice and goose bumps breaking out on every part of my body. On the other side of me was Chuddah, although I didn't know yet he was Chuddah. I just thought of him as the big black boy with arms like cold slabs of meat linked into mine.

There were 164 of us in that surf line that summer, Indoc SEAL class, the number of which is classified. Somewhere between 200 and 250, is all I can say. Which meant that at least 2,000 men had done this exact same thing we were doing, and had somehow survived it.

That's what I kept reminding myself as Darhart hollered at us to turn and lie on our backs in the surf. I can't imagine what we looked like from above, still linked, turning as one unit, to put our heads at the surf line and our legs on the sand.

The first time the water came over my head, I knew I would drown. That's what you do when you look up to see this cold claw of black water coming at you. It came down over us, harder than water should be, and it filled my mouth and eyes and ears like the opposite of a deprivation chamber. With my arms linked, I couldn't let go, wouldn't let go if they didn't, and then the water went away and we spit it out and shook it from our eyes and

5

were glad to be alive.

That gladness lasted about four waves and then you wished one of those waves would just fill you so much you'd never feel the cold again. Rocks and sand bashing your skin, as bruising as the butt of a gun. Who knew that water could carry such things, could bring them down with such force?

That moment, I wished for death, maybe. Hell, I did. I can say that now. If it hadn't been for Jonas, squeezing my arm with that bicep of his, I would have gotten up to run, I would have been the first to ring that big black bell and go back to the shit hole I'd come from. But every time the water went away, Jonas was looking at me with his no-colour eyes. One time, he even tried to say something before the next wave knocked sand and seashells against our lips.

Darhart walked at our feet. I hated him for being dry. 'Let's hear you,' he said.

No one wanted to start. The call seemed stupid, a grade school game.

'If I don't hear you, you're out.'

Next to me, Jonas started the howl. His "hoo-ya" was louder than I could have imagined, and it only took seconds for others to answer him. I found my own voice joining them until the surf busted in and washed the howl from my lips. As soon as I could breathe, I started again. It felt good, like a fuck-you to Darhart, to our own bodies' needs, to the ocean itself.

After a while, I became nothing but rhythm; the slowed-down beat of my sluggish blood. There was eternity in every crash of water, purpose in every inhale and sound. Jonas' hoo-ya in my ears and my own howl in response.

Darhart's voice surprised me out of the place I'd gone.

'Sand dunes!'

We ran to the sand dunes still linked together, our own giant wave of wet men. But we rolled alone. Rolled ourselves in the sand until our boots, our trousers, our T-shirts, our hair, our ears and eyes were full of sand. Sugar cookies, they called it. I've never been able to eat them since. Just looking at them on a plate makes me feel the grit of sand squeaking between my teeth.

With Jonas and Chuddah on either side of me, we did that cycle – water and sand – five times straight. Five times and my gut felt like it was ready to puke out everything it ever had down it. My face was so cold I didn't know if I was still wearing it. Chuddah was shivering on one side of me. When a man that big shivered, and his arms were linked with yours, you shivered too. You more than shivered; you shook so hard your teeth clunked together. Even if you weren't already shaking on your own, which I was.

At the end of sugar cookie roll five, we stood. My skin chafed and burned inside the wet rough of my clothes. My teeth and eyes were full of sand. My belly contracted and threatened to heave. There's pain that makes sense, and pain that doesn't. And then there's pain that's beyond thinking. This was that kind of pain, and it was still the beginning.

'Steel it out,' Jonas said. I don't know how he could even move his lips. Mine were so cold they could only press together to try and keep my guts inside.

He put his hand on my shoulder. Big hand. Maybe hot, maybe cold. I couldn't feel a damn thing. But where his attention had helped me through the surf line, now I wanted to punch him. Him, standing in front of me not shaking at all. Able to smile even though I could see the sand between his front teeth. I thought he was the kind of man who would make it through Indoc. And I was pretty sure that meant I was the kind of man who wouldn't.

I wanted Jonas from that first day in surf-training. I can say that now. Jonas was the reason I stayed, the reason I made it, not just through surf training, but later, when things got harder. I didn't know why Jonas stayed. I liked to imagine that it was because of me. But I think he stayed because it was the only thing he knew how to do.

I fucked Jonas in my head on the long runs, on the surf and sugar cookies days. I sucked his imagined dick in my mind during drown-proofing – hours in the water with our hands and feet tied, bouncing up for air. The image of Jonas' imagined dick was sometimes all that kept me afloat.

It was the grinder, that mother-fucker of an obstacle course, that finally brought us together. Two weeks in and we hit it: parallel bars, jumping over shit, jogging on rolling logs, a 40-foot-high cargo net. You name it. If they could dream it up, they had us going over it, under it or staying upright on it.

The rope swing was what hung me up. Jonas and I were in the back. Jonas because he liked to stick back and catch up with everyone halfway through the pack. I was there because Jonas was there.

I was a skinny boy then. Strong, but skinny. Could hold my breath and body underwater for ages. Could run down a beach and back a 100 times. But that rope swing. Damned if I could pull myself up it. First time, I ran at it, full speed, hauled myself a third of the way up and landed on my ass in the sand.

Darhart stalked behind us.

'Try it again,' he said.

'Fuck off,' Jonas said, quiet. I knew Darhart could hear

him, but Jonas was like that. He could get away with things.

I tried that rope eight, nine times. I told myself I could do it, and every time I ended up on my ass in the sand. I couldn't feel my palms any more, but I could smell the rope burning through my skin. The rope began to turn red-brown where I grabbed it.

Darhart motioned toward the pickup that followed up everywhere, carrying Mama Moy's Black Bell. Three rings on that big black bell and you could leave, no questions asked. The palms on my hands bleeding into the sand made that black bell look good, made it look like home. Better than home.

I made a step toward the bell, so dark and solid in the sunlight, and it was Jonas who put his hand on my shoulder. I couldn't look into his no-colour eyes, so different from the blood on my hands. 'Steel it out,' he said out loud. Softer, so I could barely hear him, he said, 'Steel it out for me.'

I did. I steeled it out for Jonas, for his eyes and the way his dick looked in my head when I was underwater, and I made it to the top of that bastard of a rope.

That night, Jonas came to me. So quiet I didn't hear him, even though I was already wake-dreaming of him in my bunk, my hand covering my hard-on.

'Come with me,' he whispered. He pulled me from my bed and through the dark room.

Men stirred around us in their bunks. I knew they could hear, but no one spoke. Because it was Jonas.

I followed him into the night in my boxers, bare feet stepping forward without thinking. In the dark, the Grinder took on new shapes, more solid, more real.

'Hands on the rope,' he said, when we reached it.

9

I put my hands up, felt the rope burn into my tender palms.

In the silent dark, Jonas' mouth was the soft surf sliding over mine; a kinder surf than what I'd known these last two weeks, but not much. He used his teeth on my lips, biting hard until I thought I tasted blood, but I didn't know if it was from earlier, from the way I'd licked my palms after, like a cat.

He bit his way down the front of me until he reached my boxers. His breath came through the fabric, and then his fingers were against my hips, pulling down the shorts. My dick bounced up against the cold air, searching.

He made me lick his palm, each of his fingers, until his hand was wet. He reached down and rubbed my saliva over the head of his dick.

'Don't let go,' he said.

I couldn't answer, so I just shook my head in the dark.

His fingers entered me. He wasn't slow or kind, and I was glad. My hands hurt like hell, and now my lip. And I'd almost rang that big fucking bell and gone back to my hell-hole of a life. I'd nearly fucked up. I wanted him to make me feel pain somewhere, anywhere, else.

And he did. The tip of his dick against my ass was only pressure at first, and then it was wet pain. The same as my hands, only focused. A knife pressing against the well of vein until it splits. And then there was only pressure and the light-headed white pain that comes from opening yourself up.

I kept my hands on the rope, held on as strong as I could. His slide into me wasn't slow, but it was sure. It was metal and rod and then Jonas' dick in my ass hitting that spot so far up that it was like the knot at the top of the highest rope. His balls slapping against me. The whole of me tight and loose in waves. The rhythm of it. There was

10

eternity in every stroke. And then Jonas crashed into me, his teeth clenched in my shoulder, whispering 'hoo-ya' until I came, a shuddering exhale.

Eight weeks of Indoc, of Sugar Cookie Summer, we steeled it out together, Jonas and me. And when someone finally broke, and rang the black bell, it wasn't me. But by then, Jonas was steeling it out with someone else – with Chuddah – and I was wishing it had been me who'd rang that black fucker of a bell.

Whatever they tell you about becoming a SEAL, whatever they write in the papers and whisper during war time, it's true, but it's not the whole story. It is harder that I can even tell, after all these years. It made me believe in super heroes and the strength of gritting through, at a time when I didn't believe in anything. Less than half of our guys made it. I made it. I made it by waiting every night for Jonas to come back to my bed. But he never did.

Now, with him bound in front of me, in the uniform of the other guys, looking up at me with those fucking eyes out of my past, I know he's come for me again.

I put my dick back in my pants. My hands shake around the zipper. I pull the hood off and there's Jonas. His hair's a little darker now and there are frown lines across his forehead, but it's him. The man I loved so many years ago.

'What the fuck, Jonas? What the fuck are you doing here?'

'Same thing you are.' He laughs, a short bark. 'Trying to catch the bad guy.'

He looks up at me and shakes his head. 'Fuck, I thought I was done for. All this time, I'd been thinking you were that fucker I came to kill. That fucking BB guy.'

He eyes my crotch. 'Lucky I didn't bite that thing off. I

11

was seriously thinking about it.'

Jonas is saying all the right things, but there's something in his eyes. He's trying to figure it out. Me, I've figured it out. But I don't let on.

'Shit,' I say. I put my hand over my dick. It's still half-hard, and the front of my pants are damp. 'So you're here after BB?'

He nods. 'Agency can't get their act together. Sends in two of its best men, but doesn't tell either of them? Stupid.'

'Stupid,' I agree. I knew they'd send someone after me, but I didn't expect it to be Jonas.

I look into Jonas' pale-pale eyes. He's waiting for me to cut him free. He doesn't know; he hasn't figured out that we're not on the same side. I have to let him up. I owe him at least that. I lean over him and slide my knife through the rope. 'I'm sorry about this,' I say as I give him my hand.

'No worries,' he says. He barely pulls on my hand as he gets to his feet. 'Now we'll catch the fuck ...'

For the first time, Jonas sees my wrist, the heavy black bell tattooed across the back of it. A perfect replica; I had it done in Asia from the mental photo in my head.

'Black Bell,' he whispers. 'You're ... BB.'

He's still good. His elbow slides through my defences and knocks against my windpipe and I cough, hard and fast. He's better than me, still, probably. But I get my knife into his side even as he knocks me sideways. And in the end, I'm the one with steel in my hand and steel in my heart. Jonas taught me that.

Beauty and the Beast
by Penelope Friday

Len rang the buzzer at the house and waited for Sebastian to answer, his heart thudding uncomfortably, as it always did.

'Yes?' Sebastian's drawl echoed through the intercom.

'It's me.' *It is I*, Sebastian had told him so many times, was the correct grammar. Len listened, nodded seriously, and continued to use his own form of words.

'Come in.'

The burr of the door unlocking, that so familiar sound. Len must have heard it hundreds of times in the past. Sebastian had never offered him a key; Len had never asked for one. He pushed against the door and let himself in; took his boots off and put them neatly on the shoe rack before climbing the stairs to find Sebastian.

'I'm in the kitchen,' his lover called, and Len strolled, hands in pockets, into the large, gadget-driven room.

'Cooking?' Len asked.

Sebastian raised one eyebrow at the improbable suggestion.

'Opening wine. Sit down.' He indicated the oak bench that stood by the kitchen window, and Len slumped down onto it. 'So, my dear, how are you?'

'Fine. Long day,' said Len concisely. 'You?'

'Oh.' Sebastian made a little moue with his lips, his

13

hands busy on the corkscrew. The cork came out of the wine bottle with a pop. 'As well as ever, if a little dull. However, I can at least look forward to tomorrow. I have nothing on until a lunch engagement. My morning is my own.'

'Mine isn't. I can't stay,' Len said quietly.

'I haven't asked you to.'

'No.'

Sebastian hadn't asked him to stay the night. Never would. Not because he didn't want him to stay, but because he couldn't bear the thought of being turned down. And Len would turn him down – they both knew that. Not because he didn't want to stay, didn't love Sebastian, but because ... oh, because their lives were so very different that they had scarcely a single point in common.

Theirs was a pointless, hopeless, relationship leading nowhere.

Sebastian was – one of the Fortesque-Lloyds, one of the richest, oldest families in the country, with everything that their name stood for. Was blue blooded; a proud, arrogant man who believed that there was no one as important – as good – as his Family. His days were spent in luxurious idleness, in engagements with other important families. What Sebastian described as work was time spent at charity fund-raisers, paying sums that Len could only dream of in order to attend dances or suppers with all the people he saw every week anyway.

Len was – a carpenter. Having said that, considering Sebastian's background, there was perhaps no need to say more. A gay carpenter. Sebastian at least had the distinction of loving (and sleeping with? Probably: Len knew better than to ask a question that he didn't want the answer to) women as well. Len loved no one but

Sebastian. Not like *that*. And yet it was Len who refused to stay; Len who put the limits on their relationship. Len, whose soul was bound to an entirely different set of ideals – to the ideas of service, hard work and graft – even whilst his heart was Sebastian's alone.

The Family (always spelt in Len's mind – and, he suspected, in Sebastian's – with a capital F), the Fortesque-Lloyds, were never mentioned when Sebastian and Len were alone, though Len was aware of their presence at almost all times. The only place in the entire building that they did not haunt was the bedroom: when Sebastian and Len made love, there was no room for anyone else in word, thought or deed. They belonged to each other, in total oneness.

'You'll have a drink whilst you're here, I presume,' Sebastian said. 'You're not leaving immediately?'

Len nodded. Sebastian poured him a glass of white wine and passed it to him. He had no need to ask Len what he wanted, any more than Len had needed to answer the question. They knew each other, these two: knew their habits, their likes – dislikes – failings – thoughts. Len sipped the drink. Sebastian would allow him three sips before suggesting that he might like to sit somewhere more comfortable. They would start on the sofa; Sebastian would take Len's glass from him – sniff it, sip it, savour the taste. Then he would kiss him.

'So how was your day today? Any reason for the dullness?' Sometimes, Len thought, they had the stilted conversation of total strangers. But it was harder still than that: there were so many things that could not – must not – be said; that hung unspoken in the air between them.

Sebastian shrugged elegantly.

'No more than usual. Yourself?'

'The same.'

15

Len took that third sip, and Sebastian looked over at him.

'Is there really any need to sit in the kitchen as if we were servants?' he asked laconically. 'Would we not be more comfortable somewhere else?'

'Where do you suggest?'

'The drawing room, perhaps?'

Len had once teased Sebastian for the pretentious use of "drawing room" rather than "living room" or "lounge" as most people would have called it. Whenever Sebastian said the words now, there was a slight spark of amusement in his eyes.

'The drawing room sounds great.' The spark was reflected in Len's smile.

To begin with, Len had always felt a little uncomfortable in the luxurious surroundings of Sebastian's London pad. He had sat on the edge of the leather sofa, realising the full extent of the difference between their ways of life. Len spent his days scrabbling round for a job, any job. His profession was on its way out, and his undeniable ability did not change the cruel facts. Today had included being turned down for several artisanal projects which would have guaranteed his being able to afford to eat for the next month or two.

Sebastian ... Sebastian had no idea what it was to have money difficulties. His "job" was being a Fortesque-Lloyd, an aristocrat. They lived in the same city but inhabited different worlds. Len knew that if he ever told Sebastian that he was short of cash, his lover would have provided for him without a second thought. But there were some things that were sacred. At the moment – OK, Len and Sebastian occupied different positions in society, but the relationship between them was equal. Neither man was beholden to the other: each gave as much as his lover.

That was what Len wanted; that was right. He would accept Sebastian's wine, accept his hospitality, but not his money. Never that. He managed, and he kept his self-respect: could face himself in the mirror each morning.

Over time, however, Len had accepted – grown accustomed to, even – their different styles of living. Had known that, despite the pleasure he got from being surrounded by such beauty and opulence, he would never have felt at home here. The bed-sit he rented on the other side of London, while not the sort of place he could ever have taken Sebastian, was nevertheless "home" in a way that this expensive apartment could never be. He leant back now against the smooth leather sofa, his right side touching Sebastian's left from knee to shoulder, revelling in that touch.

'Is the wine satisfactory?' Sebastian asked.

He put out his hand, and Len, smiling, handed him the glass. Sebastian swirled the liquid around the crystal cut wineglass, brought it to his nose, and then finally took the smallest of delicate mouthfuls.

'It will do, I think,' said Len quietly. 'Don't you?'

And Sebastian's lips were on his, the glass put gently but firmly down on the occasional table by the side of the sofa. Len could feel his heart already beating faster at the first touch of Sebastian's mouth, of Sebastian's hands on his body. They had been lovers for three years, and Len still had no idea what it was that Sebastian saw in him: the handsome, blond aristocratic Sebastian Fortesque-Lloyd and the dark-haired, scarred carpenter Len Price – the beauty and the beast. Len surrendered himself into the kiss, his arms encircling Sebastian; and his lover said, as was his way,

'I think the bedroom might suit our needs, Len.'

Len never had words to answer this; instead his hands

were still clutching at Sebastian's clothes as they shifted themselves into the sumptuous bedroom, his mouth fusing back onto Sebastian's as soon as the other man had finished speaking. Sebastian guided them both to the bed, rolling Len onto it and lying on top of him on the more-than-king-sized bed.

'Sebastian ... Sebastian ...' Len heard himself mumbling, as his fingers fumbled with the buttons that separated him from his lover. 'God, I want you.'

'Len.' And the sound of Sebastian's voice was a caress, more intimate than any gesture he could make as he took Len's name and made it his own property, just as Len was his.

Len dug his fingers sharply into Sebastian's skin, marking him as his own. Later, he would wonder whether he could not help himself, or whether it was his way of claiming Sebastian, so that every other person Sebastian might (or might not) fuck would know that they weren't alone, that this man belonged to another. Sebastian never complained: at this moment he was arching into Len, his cock rubbing hotly against Len's thigh as he pushed warm hands under Len's T-shirt, forcing it up and over his head. Len shrugged it off, gave up the gentle approach and ripped at Sebastian's shirt, regardless of the buttons, so that they lay chest to bare chest. Sebastian pulled back a little, his eyes seeking Len's, and he smiled a little as Len put firm hands around his arse, dispensing with his trousers before pulling him closer than before.

And they were naked, and Len could feel the hurried beat of Sebastian's pulse; knew that – for some inexplicable reason – he was as important, as desirable, to Sebastian as Sebastian was to him. Knew that this was the one place where there was no doubt of their equality; that like called to like as they groaned and rubbed against each other. Knew, as he rolled Sebastian over, slithered down his body, his mouth closing around Sebastian's cock, that this need, this hunger was all for him, that it was …

'Ah, God, Len,' Sebastian cried.

… was a mystery, perhaps *the* mystery of life; and yet that at the same time it didn't matter, nothing mattered but the feel of their bodies; the sound; the smell; the taste that was so purely Sebastian. Oh yes, especially that salty, sexual taste that made Len want to come without even being touched himself.

His lover had his head thrown back; was running his fingertips gently (so different to the fierce, desperate need of Len's own touch) over Len's shoulders as Len made love to him. Len knelt between his legs, the feel of Sebastian's erect cock in his mouth almost overwhelming his senses as he swirled his tongue around the head, took Sebastian deep, deep into his throat. Then, before he came, Sebastian pulled him up beside him, and was kissing him over and over again with a passion that had grown, not lessened, with every time they did this. And Sebastian was reaching a frustrated hand to find the lube; his voice whispering things he would never say at any other time to Len – dirty things, sexy things *'Please, please, fuck me. Screw me into the bed. I want to be your slut, Len'.*

Wanting, wanting, *needing* him. Len took the tube from Sebastian's clutch, squirted the cold liquid onto his hand and smoothed it on his cock. And Sebastian's body opened for him as he pressed gently, then with a firmness and determination that had Sebastian groaning and crying his name.

'Len, Len, ah God, there Len, yes – yes, there. Fuck …'

They were consumed by each other, even as they fucked. Nothing else mattered.

Nothing else mattered, but one thing had changed. For afterwards, as they lay together on the bed, at last Sebastian said it. Those final, fateful words.

'Len … Stay.'

How Many Times is the First Time?
by Chrissie Bentley

I don't think anybody was really sure whether or not Marty was gay – or cared, for that matter. He was nice enough, but he wasn't going to win any awards for the hottest boy in the office, either.

I thought he was cute the first time I saw him, though, and we were going out for after-work drinks within a few days of my starting at the company. But even when a few beers before we caught our buses turned into meals before the occasional night at the movies or a club, any secret fancies that Marty may have been harbouring never raised their head – and I never said a word. Which, considering we were both well into our 30s, probably strikes you as a little odd.

He was so easy to get along with, though, that it really didn't seem to matter whether we ever went any further. Occasionally, we'd discuss past relationships, but in the kind of general way that kept us both guessing – "my old partner ..." this. "My former lover ..." that. We could have been discussing household appliances for all the humanity and gender we invested in our descriptions. We'd been hanging out together for about three months when I locked myself out of my apartment. It was my own stupidity, as these things usually are – waking late and racing out, I slammed the front door before realising my keys were still on the dressing table.

After half an hour spent fruitlessly trying to break back into my own home, and another hour waiting for the landlord to arrive with a spare set, I wound up spending the rest of the morning getting my own duplicates cut, then wondering who to give them to. Marty was simply the most obvious choice. If I was going to lock myself out again, at least I'd know there was another key at work.

Time passed. We were still going out after work three or four times a week, still fencing around any subject that even threatened to introduce any intimacy to our friendship. And then, one morning, I awoke to hear Marty "hallo-ing" from the kitchen. More than a little puzzled, I pulled on a robe and padded out there. 'What....?'

'Oh my God, I'm such an idiot. This time I locked myself out!' He'd run out to buy some milk and cigarettes – and the same thing. Slammed the doors, forgot his keys, and ... here he was. 'Well, it was either go to the coffee shop and drink my first cup with a load of strangers, or come round here and have it with you.' And then he stopped. 'Uh ... you may want to run and put some shorts on. Or are you just very pleased to see me?'

I glanced down to where Marty's eyes were resting. My robe was still tightly tied at the waist. But that early morning hard-on that we all wake up to find was pushing at the fabric regardless. He laughed. 'Still, at least you're never going to lose something that size,' and his voice suddenly sounded strangely questioning, 'I was beginning to wonder about you.'

How do you respond to something like that? You were beginning to wonder? In what way? I tried to deliver a witty reply, but of course there were none to be found, just a murmured, 'No, all present and correct,' as I willed my willie to behave itself. Excusing myself for a moment,

22

I went back into the bedroom, pulled on some briefs and trousers, and the kettle was boiling by the time I got back. Crisis averted.

Or was it? Two or three times during the day, I caught Marty glancing over at me with what looked like a faint smile playing about his lips; and two or three times, too, I felt a stirring … no. It was a long time since any guy had commented on the size of my dick, but it didn't mean he wanted to actually do anything with it. I resolved to bide my time, and see if he raised the subject again. Sometimes, my patience astonishes me.

A normal evening passed between us – a drink, a meal, a walk around the stores. Standing at the bus stop, though, he suddenly let slip an almost violent, 'oh, shit.'

'What?'

'I've only gone and forgotten my keys again. They're still in my fucking desk.'

I looked at my watch – heaven knows why; the office locked up when we left. There'd be no one there 'til morning. 'What are you going to do?'

'Oh, I don't know.' He sighed loudly. 'How comfortable's your couch?'

'OK, I guess ... no, it's fine. It's yours. Come on. You can even have another cup of coffee.'

All the way home on the bus, my mind was racing. Did he deliberately forget his keys? Did he really want to sleep on the couch? Should I offer him the bed and take the couch myself? I hoped not – I was lying when I said it was fine. There were more lumps in that thing than a vat of cottage cheese. Which meant the smartest, kindest solution would be for us both to ... yes, but I didn't even want to think about that right now. He'd already spotted one inadvertent stiffy; another one, and who knows what he'd think. Or would he? Those smiles, that laugh, that

23

question.

The bus stopped and we walked the few yards to my apartment. At the door, digging into my pocket for my keys, I felt my hand brush Marty's ass. No big deal, I'm sure that wasn't the first time I'd done it. But this time, I noticed; and, from his intake of breath, so did he.

Once inside, I did it again, as I helped him off with his coat. Clumsier, this time, though; accidentally on purpose, and there was no reaction at all. Damn. I put the kettle on.

'Coffee, this late?' he asked. 'Anyone would think you were trying to keep me awake.'

'Well ...' I admitted I'd not been strictly truthful about the couch; and he admitted he'd not been truthful about wanting to sleep on it. 'I saw that bed of yours. There's plenty of room for us both in there. You won't even know I'm there.' He paused. 'I bet your early morning visitor will, though.' And suddenly he was in my arms, his mouth locked against mine and his entire body pressed tight against me. I just about remembered to switch the kettle off again before we dragged one another into the bedroom and, by the time we'd undressed one another, it was clear that he knew exactly what he was doing, brushing my cock with his, his warm hardness teasing my nerve ends with exquisite tenderness.

'You don't know how many times I've dreamed of this,' I whispered, holding him close to me.

'You don't know how many times I've dreamed of a lot of things.' He smiled, his breath and then his tongue warm on one of my nipples.

I stroked his hair as he closed his lips around it, then let out a small groan as he shifted slightly, and began tracing down my stomach.

He moved slowly, almost distractedly. Light kisses, soft bites, gentle nuzzles. I felt his tongue flick inside my

24

belly button, then move sideways and linger gently on my side. His body, too, was in barely perceptible motion, shifting his weight, manoeuvring around. Turning my head, I could see his prick swaying, a sheen of pre-come catching the light from the bedside lamp. I wondered what it would taste like, but resisted the temptation. I wanted to see what he was planning, first.

Marty's mouth was lower now, kissing my stomach, just inches away from my granite-aching cock. He showed no sign of being interested in that, though; one moment he was close enough that a simple twitch would have touched his tongue, the next he was softly biting the top of my leg. Then, as his hand gently cupped my balls, he stopped and looked up at me with an expression of unfathomable innocence. 'You're probably going to think I'm an absolute idiot, but – what do I do now?'

'Nothing ... you're doing fine,' I whispered, but he didn't move.

'No, I mean ...' His hand slipped onto my shaft. 'I've never ...' Again his voice trailed away, and I suddenly understood.

'Whatever you want ... whatever you think will feel good – for both of us.' I racked my brain for the right words. How do you explain to someone how to suck your cock? 'You put it in your mouth and ....' No. I tried to play it cool. 'Kiss me again like you were doing, but this time don't cover so much ground.'

'Like this?' His lips grazed the base of my shaft, lingered for a moment, then retreated.

'Yeah, but a little harder, and a little longer.'

'Like this?' Again I felt his lips there, exactly as I said; a little harder and a little longer.

'That's it. Now keep doing that for a moment. See what I taste like; use your tongue a little.'

Obediently – that's the only word for it – he began sliding his mouth gently around, occasionally touching the top of my sac, but always stopping just short of the head of my cock.

I was rock hard by now, but his hand kept my cock pressed firmly to my belly, as his tongue began to roam more freely.

'Let it go, touch the tip,' I breathed, half-conscious of just how absurd those words sounded, but scarcely caring as his lips finally closed over the end. 'That's wonderful,' I sighed. 'Don't stop.'

'You're not going to ...'

'Come? No, not yet. I'll let you know.' Much as I would have loved to, I didn't think Marty would appreciate a mouthful of spunk this early in his apprenticeship. But, no sooner had that thought crossed my mind than I almost lost it altogether, as his lips sunk over the tip, over the head, and half my cock disappeared inside his mouth. He held me there for a moment, withdrew and then sunk down again. From the back of his throat, I heard him moan, then gasped with amazement as he licked me again, his tongue sweeping across the top of my cock, then pausing to twirl a little, as though it was trying to burrow inside the hole, and winkle out more of the pre-come that was now beginning to flow so freely.

'You like that?' His voice was dancing. 'I'm glad. Because I can't believe how delicious you are!'

His head dipped as he took half ... more than half of me into his mouth, and then his movements grew more frenzied, fuck-sucking my cock as hard as he could, pausing for a breath, tossing a loose strand of hair from his face, and then taking me deeper every time. Again, his cock was right in front of me, so close I could almost taste it, and so wet with his own clear juices that I could have

26

drunk from it. It was too late to stop myself; I reached out and grasped his ass, dragged him over my face and pulled his hardness into my mouth, sucking hard even as I forced my throat to relax around him

My nose grazed his ball bag, and he gave a little groan. But nothing was going to distract him from his new-found pleasure, nothing at all. He slipped off my face with a whispered, 'You'll get your turn in a moment. But I want to see what you really taste like.'

That was it – as his words sank in, I felt a massive orgasm welling up inside me, tightening my balls, building up the full length of my cock. Quickly, I groaned out a warning, and felt him halt his sucking long enough for the first jet of come to spurt out of me; I sensed, rather than saw it spatter on his chest, and I knew that soon, I'd be licking it off and passing it back into his mouth with my tongue. As I began to sit up, though, Marty had my cock back in his mouth, greedily drawing every last drop of spunk out of me, sucking and swallowing me dry and holding me in his mouth even as I started to soften.

'Jesus, that was amazing,' I breathed as he finally released me and clambered back up to face me. 'Are you sure that was your first time?'

He laughed out loud. 'It's always the first time with somebody new,' he replied. 'The trick is, to make sure that it always remains the first time as well. Now, hadn't you better ask me exactly how I'd like you to suck me? It's your first time as well, you know.'

It's a Sin
by Alex Jordaine

As a teenager I was a late developer sexually and, with the wisdom of hindsight, I'm sure I know why that was: I was putting off the evil day. And I use the expression advisedly.

When that day did finally arrive and I discovered the delights of masturbation, I found what I was doing a decidedly guilty pleasure. This was because I'd been raised as a Catholic – a religion that teaches that self-pleasuring is sinful. What I went on to do, though, was in a different league altogether to the solitary act of masturbation and would certainly be regarded as wicked by the Catholic Church. In fact, they would call what I did a mortal sin.

It all started on a Sunday. I was looking forward to the week ahead as it was a half term holiday. As usual I was attending Mass, but instead of worshipping God I was on my knees worshipping the pretty blond altar server who was assisting the priest with the service.

His name was Jerry and he was a year older than me. He lived nearby with his widowed mother. She and my mother were friendly through their involvement with the Church but Jerry and I were only passing acquaintances. On this occasion, though, as our mothers talked to one another after the service, Jerry and I also got into conversation and were getting on really well.

'What are you doing this week?' I asked.

'I've nothing planned,' he replied. 'How about the two of us going swimming tomorrow afternoon?'

I said I thought this was a good idea and we made arrangements to meet.

That night, I couldn't resist the temptation to masturbate as I imagined what Jerry might look like without clothes – I was about to find that out, and a hell of a lot more besides.

We got together the next day and made our way to the nearby open-air swimming pool. As we walked along, chatting about this and that, I allowed my gaze to wander up and down Jerry's body. I couldn't help thinking how good he looked in his skin-tight jeans. I admired the perfect shape of his rear, moulded into the faded denim, and the impressive bulge at the front.

Although the weather was reasonably mild that day, there were a lot of wet-looking clouds in the sky, and when we arrived we found that the pool was only sparsely attended. There was a slight breeze that ruffled the water, which looked downright cold. We went into the changing rooms and, at Jerry's suggestion, shared a cubicle. As he stripped off, I was surprised – and turned on – to notice that he hadn't been wearing any underwear beneath those tight jeans. I was aware that my cock was starting to swell when I slipped into my swimming trunks, and found it a decided relief – an embarrassment averted – to run on ahead and plunge into the chilly water of the swimming pool.

Jerry and I stayed in the pool for about an hour, splashing about, and it gradually warmed up. Every once in a while the sun even deigned to reveal itself through a break in the clouds, allowing reflected light to dance on the rippling blue water. Jerry and I swam and played in the pool – and, OK, maybe we did make physical contact a bit more than was strictly necessary in our games there.

When we got out of the water the changing room was empty apart from ourselves. We dried off in the same cubicle, still in our swimming costumes. However, our bulges were becoming increasingly pronounced and when I took off my swimming trunks my cock sprang out erect.

'Mmm, that looks very nice,' said Jerry, who pulled down his trunks to reveal his own lengthening erection. 'Come on,' he said, his member now as full and stiff as my own. 'Let's jerk off together.'

Feeling light-headed and extremely excited, I encircled my erect cock with my fingers as I watched Jerry bring a hand to his own erection. We both rubbed our cocks up and down vigorously, climaxing at pretty much the same time. And equally lavishly too, spraying out streams of sticky wetness onto each other with great force. It was an amazing feeling, it truly was – my first time masturbating with anyone else, and the most intense sexual experience that I'd so far had in my young life.

Jerry and I showered, dried ourselves, dressed and headed for home, both of us more than a little subdued. We said very little as we strode along, lost in our own guilty thoughts. Just as we were about to part, however, Jerry brightened. 'Fancy coming round to my house tomorrow?' he said. He told me that his mother would be at work all day so we'd have the place to ourselves.

'That'd be great,' I replied.

'It's a date, then. See you around 11 a.m.' Jerry's face suddenly broadened into a devilish grin. 'Hey, and no more jerking off until then.'

That proved easier said than done. I fidgeted about uneasily in my bed that night. My mind was in a whirl going over and over what Jerry and I had done together and what might happen tomorrow. According to my Church all these "impure thoughts" were a sin but the feelings of guilt this caused just seemed to make my cock harder. I was excited as much as anything by the intoxicating shame of my own arousal. Even so, although it took a deal of willpower, I didn't touch myself that night.

The next day I killed time earlier in the morning trying to decide what to wear for my "date". A clean white T-shirt and one of my pairs of jeans, I thought. On a whim, I removed my underwear, taking a leaf out of Jerry's book, and squeezed into the oldest, and, more to the point, tightest pair of jeans I possessed.

I set off, slightly nervous but very excited, the knot in my stomach no competition for the throbbing of my shaft. My growing sense of anticipation and the rough feel of the tight denim against my cock meant that I was in a high state of sexual arousal by the time I arrived at Jerry's house.

When he answered the door I was struck anew by how devastatingly attractive he was, with his blond hair falling over his forehead; that pretty face and lithe, athletic body. He was wearing nothing but the faded jeans he'd worn the day before, which clung to his form like a second skin.

'Hi there, you're looking good,' he said, reaching over and squeezing the bulge in my own skin-tight jeans. I did the same to him, feeling the warmth of his cock beneath the straining denim.

'Would you like a coffee or anything else to drink?' he asked.

'No thanks, I'm fine,' I replied.

'You sure are,' he said with another devilish grin. 'Follow me, we'll go up to my room and fool around.'

Once in his bedroom we hastily stripped and were soon on his bed mutually masturbating, our excitement growing and growing. We climaxed simultaneously in great bursting spurts, and then lay together in the afterglow, the come on our bellies intermingling.

We washed ourselves and put on our jeans, then went and had a snack in the kitchen and just hung out for a while around the house. But it wasn't long before our lust erupted again and our swelling members were straining once more against the tight denim that covered them. We were soon naked and erect again in his bedroom, masturbating each other feverishly. And for most of the rest of that afternoon we simply couldn't keep our hands off each other.

'How about tomorrow?' asked Jerry, as I was about to leave.

'You bet,' I replied eagerly.

It seemed like an eternity to me until we met the next day. I reckon Jerry must have felt much the same way because as soon as he'd let me into the house and shut the front door he pulled me towards him and kissed me hard. I kissed him right back, savouring the slick, demanding feel of his lips and frantic tongue, and reciprocating for all I was worth. Jerry and I carried on kissing passionately while rubbing our bulging cocks together, getting more and more turned on. We then went up to his room, stripped naked again and began mutually masturbating once more. Then the mood changed ...

'Kneel down,' Jerry said all of a sudden, his tone chilly with command. I obeyed in an instant. 'Now suck me off,' he added, 'and make a good job of it.'

I was determined to do just that. I engulfed his stiff cock with my lips – it tasted so good, I can't tell you – and swirled my tongue around its swollen head. My tongue laved his cock, licking the thickness, my lips kissing and rubbing against it so that it flexed and strained against my mouth. Next, I began sucking on his shaft with slow regular movements, then faster, then slower, then faster still. I felt as if I was born to give blow jobs. It made me feel deliciously wicked, thoroughly debauched and perverted and sinful.

After I'd been blowing Jerry for a while he announced, 'I'm going to climax real soon now.' His voice was full of sexual tension but just as commanding as before. 'When I do,' he added, 'I want you to swallow my come, every last drop.'

I wanted to do that too, craved it. The thought of it made me shiver with pleasure. I could taste the beads of liquid seeping constantly from the slit of his cock and knew that they would soon be a gushing torrent. Then it happened. Jerry emitted a strangled moan and erupted to a shuddering orgasm, his cock gushing wad after wad of creamy come deep into my mouth. And I did exactly as I'd been told. My head still furiously pumping, I drew down every ounce of the semen that spurted onto the back of my tongue, taking it deep into my throat – every last drop of it.

There's not a lot to add to my story after that. Jerry and I carried on meeting in the same way for the rest of that half term week. And the following Sunday saw me at Mass on my knees again, my cock pulsing constantly as I worshipped that beautiful blond altar server. As a devout Roman Catholic I knew what I was feeling and what I'd done was sinful and wicked in the extreme, but I just couldn't help myself. I felt so guilty about it all, I really did. And the guilt I felt was delicious.

Snow Wolf
by John Connor

In my mind I can still see the snow, vast masses of snow, and pine trees – forest for mile upon square mile. It was deep in Mother Russchkya at the start of the winter, November 1905, and it was a time of chaos and uncertainty. The Mensheviks were already beginning to form up and the Revolution was starting to take shape. The supposed bloody joys of politics in reality turned people against each other.

But all of that was of little or no concern to me. I had my forest cabin, my traps, my fish lines and my small herd of goats. Let them have their Revolution, for all the good it will do them! I had chosen my life, out of necessity and harsh social pressures, and if truth be known, as a young man I no longer cared for high finance and the power of the Rouble. I had finally found peace and fulfilment, albeit in the form of my now simple life.

That was, until the day I found Valentin.

I had been out as early as I could manage in the cold, grey, half-light of November, dressed as heavily as I could manage in dark fox and black summer rabbit furs, and with a pair of light cross-country snow shoes bound to my feet. Regardless of the season and the weather I always had my daily routines. Checking the beaver traps for possible furs, keeping track of the larger predators during their migrations, and checking the trails for fresh winter hares. So it was that I had completed almost two thirds of the way round my circular route, when I found the abandoned horse wandering aimlessly in a tiny forest clearing I usually visit when gathering kindling.

It was a glossy, dark black beast of fine stock – far too good for forest peasants – but it was clear from the marked state of the saddle and the general distressed and agitated condition of the animal itself that its rider had been through a skirmish of some kind.

My interest piqued, I decided to find out more, and on backtracking the horse's trail I eventually came across the fallen cavalry soldier half buried in a snow drift.

Even from a distance he looked to be in his mid to late 20s, and although he appeared to be of a fair height, the bright blue, red and gold colours of his uniform made him appear almost doll-like and artificial when set against the white snow and dark pine trunks. Nor did it help that his face and hands had taken on the grey and ashen colour of unglazed porcelain.

I kept my distance rather than immediately rush to his aid, unsure for a moment if he was still alive or if he had frozen to death during the night. But when I finally detected the shallow rise and fall of his chest I moved closer – though cautiously, in case he should wake and attempt to protect himself with a pistol or a knife. As I looked more closely I could see there was blood and torn cloth, high on the upper arm of his uniform jacket, telling me immediately that he had been shot close to the shoulder. There was also a visible line of dried blood which had flowed and trickled from under his headgear, down across his forehead, and which had finally pooled in the curve of his nose. Gently I loosened the chinstraps and mindful of the low bullet hole, lifted the Ushanka away, and was quite startled and a little surprised by his head of short cut, almost pure white blond hair.

Thankfully, on closer examination of his scalp, I easily found the shallow groove where the bullet had just grazed his head as it had passed through his decorative hat.

Yet, even though he did not appear to be badly or fatally wounded, it didn't stop me worrying about his shallow breathing and deathly pallor. He was obviously suffering from exposure and needed to be carefully warmed – otherwise the sudden temperature change would as surely kill him as if he had been left out to freeze in the forest.

So, despite my vow of solitude, I quickly gathered him up in my arms, carefully placed him across the saddle of his mount, and started to head back to the protection of my cabin.

It took me less than 40 minutes to return and, after some quick rearrangements I managed to safely stable the horse with my own bewildered livestock. Yet, when I had again gathered up the injured horse-soldier and was making my way to my cabin, I thought for a moment that I felt him move in my arms, and utter 'krawtkee meeshka,' *(gentle bear)* before slipping back into unconsciousness.

But the Devil makes fools of us through our idle imaginings, and once inside I placed him carefully on the floor, then hung my coats back over the door to help keep out the bitter winter cold. With little time to lose, I quickly set about creating a makeshift hospital bed by clearing off the large wooden table in the centre of the cabin. Once done, I carefully placed the young cavalryman on top of it and pulled them both a little nearer the main fire.

With some more wood thrown on to liven up the

embers and coals a little, I turned around and, with the aid of several large oil lamps and the now brightening firelight, I started to hesitantly undress him, repeatedly checking for other less obvious wounds or other signs of damage he might have suffered in his flight through the forests.

As I gently undid the collar of his colourful outer tunic I became aware of just how handsome and distinguished he looked.

With his face passive and relaxed, although still ashen, it seemed as if he was without worry – his features clean cut, but with hints of good humour to the upturned corners of his mouth. At one time his nose had been broken and not reset cleanly, and it had left him with a slight ridge, though probably only noticeable from close up – which seemed to add, rather than detract, from his good looks.

Dismissing the distraction I unbuttoned the rest of the heavy uniform jacket fully and with some trepidation I carefully manoeuvred his arms out of it – all the time fearful that any awkward movements would cause his wound to open and start bleeding again. Thankfully it didn't, and on examining the sleeve of his undergarment, I was relieved to find it to be merely another scratch, barely cutting the skin in fact, with the blood having seeped into the wet cloth and spread like ink on a damp blotter.

Appraising him again it was clear some colour was starting to return to his face and hands, and his breathing had become deeper and more regular – a good sign that he was starting to recover strongly from his ordeal.

Encouraged by the good signs, I pulled the table nearer still to the open fire before I started to remove his black leather riding boots and icy woollen socks, carefully checking for signs of frostbite as I massaged his feet for a moment. The fine leather boots could possibly be saved as well, but as I put them down beside the table leg I realised his thick serge uniform trousers were still partially stiff with ice and heavy with water where the ice had thawed. Instinctively, I carefully undid the buttons of his thick serge trousers, unhooked them from the front of his braces, and then gently removed the rest of his uniform.

Seeing him lying on the tabletop, dressed only in his one-piece undergarment, with the shadows from the firelight jumping and flickering across his prone form, made me realise just how fragile and helpless he was. And again just how handsome and attractive I found him to be, with his head of white hair, pale blond eyebrows, small imperfect nose.

From deep within me I could feel the old stirrings slowly coming back to the surface again. The longing I had always had to feel the love of another man …

I shook my head and came back to the present. He still needed to be warmed if he was going to survive the rest of the day.

Collecting a large bowl from a nail in the cabin wall, I moved over to the fireplace. With a protective rag wrapped around my hand I lifted the ever-ready kettle from the fire's edge, and poured out some hot water – cooling it down with some clean river water in a bucket I kept by the door. If the goats got thirsty then they could have as much snow as they liked.

Taking a fresh cotton cloth from the line above the fireplace, I put everything on the table and proceeded to remove his torn and blood-stained underwear.

As I slowly unbuttoned the combinations I felt my hands start to tremble as they neared his groin, and I averted my eyes for a moment or two before returning to the top. Gently lifting his shoulders up slightly, I worked the sodden material downwards and carefully slipped him out of the top half – before going down to his feet and gently tugging the remains of the garment off him completely. Unravelling it, I put it on the line above the fireplace – out of harm's way so it could dry out overnight.

As I turned around – try as I might – I could not resist the temptation to look at this young man's totally naked body. He was trim, but not overly muscular, and it was easy for me to tell that unlike my somewhat large and now peasant-like personage, his five-foot-nine frame had not known real manual labour. The strikingly white hair on his head was also visible as fine, soft hair on his chest. I let my gaze slowly move downwards, following the white blond trail down the centre of his stomach, down and further down to his groin where it blossomed into a thick, ivory nest of pubic hair. In the midst of it was his ice-shrunken cock and tightly contracted scrotum.

Begone! I have no time for such thoughts!

I shook my head and mind back to the present, and dipping the cloth into the warm water, I wrung it out and then started to gently work some warmth and circulation back into his body.

Starting with his face, I softly sponged the dried blood from his forehead, nose and cheek, marvelling again at the colouration of his eyebrows in comparison to my dark and hirsute forearms. Rinsing the cloth in the water again, I lightly traced it over his sensuous lips, brushing my thumb across his lower lip, before moving the cloth and my hand down over his neck and shoulders, then spreading them both out across his chest.

Impulsively I scooped up a handful of warm water and let it trickle and drip though my cupped hand onto his flat stomach – watching intently as it filled his navel, then ran down over his hips in time with his breathing, to pool on the table top. Lifting the cloth from his chest I folded it several times then set about gently mopping up the water on his stomach.

Dipping the cloth to heat it up again, I wrung it out and carefully unfolded it before tentatively placing it over his groin. As gently as I could I started to slowly massage his cock and balls through the warm cloth – feeling how the heat relaxed his scrotum so that finally his balls hung freely and how much larger his cock had become under my ministrations.

Lifting back the cloth a little, I admired his manhood, and despite being dwarfed by my large hands I could see his member had already started to grow to a respectable size. In a moment of sheer recklessness I bent forwards and pressed my lips to his still steadily swelling shaft.

Straightening up again I was greeted by a pair of soft marble-green eyes looking at me with a half sleepy expression. His hand reached up, took hold of my shirt sleeve, and pulling me towards him he muttered, '*Kwratka leechnast dyeat-vyen,*' "*be gentle I am inexperienced*", before bringing his head up to kiss me firmly and without any hesitation. For a moment I was taken by surprise, but as his mouth opened to mine I abandoned all restraint and returned his unspoken question with a passionate affirmative!

Tentatively, his hand found mine and after a moment's cautious hesitation he started to guide it down over his taut flat stomach, down over his groin, and finally down between his legs, there to cup his wonderful balls.

Joyously breaking away from his mouth I recklessly planted a line of quick kisses down his chest and stomach – pausing to nuzzle into that glorious nest of white blond pubic hair – before taking his cock deep within my mouth. He let out a barely audible sigh, and as I continued to suck I could feel him start to writhe with pleasure! Moments later I felt his hand at my trousers, unbuttoning my fly and reaching in to rub at my own hard and erect cock, still trapped in my own long johns.

With his cock sliding in and out of my mouth I moved my hips around to give him better access, and his hand slid downwards to tickle and fondle my balls. *Dyeat-vyen*? He may well be *inexperienced*, but he certainly knew how to play with another man's cock! But the positions we were in were uncomfortable, and moments later I was standing, silhouetted against the fire, and while he got down off the table I proceeded to remove my own clothes, until we were standing there, totally naked, my six-foot-two, broad-shouldered frame towering above him, and with body hair as dark as his was white.

Crossing to the far side of the cabin, he stood at the foot of the large, fur-covered bed – moving aside some of the heavy blankets until only the large black bearskin was left covering the mattress. Moving onto the end of the bed he knelt down on all fours, giving me a wonderful view of his buttocks and the promises they hid from view.

With him in that position it meant I did not have to bend down far in order for me to part his warm cheeks and start to rub and run my tongue around, over and eventually into his anus. His groans of pleasure spurred me on, and in moments my saliva was heavy between his cheeks. Standing up, I took my cock in one hand and slipped it up in between his buttocks, pulling my protective foreskin back and moving myself around, in order to wet the head and shaft so as to make my entry easier for the both of us.

A little more positioning and the head was just at his

41

entrance. I put my hands on his hips and gently began to pull him backwards. I remembered my first time – Alexiaef had been brutal in his entry and I had bled like a woman for days after. I learned that it need not have been like that, and, ever since, I have been as careful and considerate as I could be with my lovers.

After a minute or so of gentle rocking and easing, I heard him gasp as my bulbous head slipped inside him. Still being careful, I gently inched the rest of my shaft into him, listening to his every sound, anxious not to hurt him too much, until my stomach was pressed firmly up against him. Taking my hands off his hips, I gently stroked the back of his neck and rubbed his shoulders and back reassuringly, whispering to him to relax, telling him how good he made me feel. As I carefully withdrew I could hear him making a curious growling sound in the back of his throat. More gentle pressure forwards and the saliva now lubricated my shaft, letting me slip more freely into him. Again, the growling at the back of his throat.

Taking that as a sign of encouragement I started to quicken my movements until I was thrusting into him, spurred on by him happily pushing backwards into my groin, his growling now louder and more open mouthed.

Spitting into the palm of my hand I reached around his hip to grasp at his cock – getting a feeling of joy at discovering it was still as hard as mine was. Holding my hand steady, I formed an open fist around his shaft, my large calloused hand dwarfing his goodly sized member, and let our movements slide his cock in and out of my fist, as if he were himself making love to another man.

In moments I could feel his cock start to twitch and his hips start to push forwards, and then he was ejaculating into my hand – spurt after spurt of hot sticky seed dribbling and oozing around my fingers, making his cock slippery and impossible to hold!

It was such a wonderful feeling, bringing such pleasure to another man, that I could no longer hold myself back – and grasping him around his slim hips I pulled him onto me, every thrust of my own hips sending my manhood further into him and finally triggering my own flood of jism, as he threw his head back and finally gave out a triumphant wolf-like howl!

After we had both rested I finished tending to his grazes and cuts, while he, between drifting in and out of much needed sleep, told me of his life so far. It was of a similar world to the one I had left behind in Tyumen City, on the banks of the Tura, and did little to encourage me back into the arms of what they now laughingly called Civilisation. But I listened to him talk of his parents, his brothers and sisters, and of a life he thought cut short when he was forced to flee from the Revolutionists, believing the bullet to be lodged in his skull, rather than having just skimmed over it.

And for a pitifully short but glorious while we became ardent lovers, hunting and working during what little day the winter gave us, then loving and sleeping through the long winter nights. And we did so unashamedly, with no peers or laws to condemn and crush our joys in having found another who trod the same be-shrouded path of love.

Time passed.

November became December, then the New Year faded into memory, and as Valentin's strength returned, so did his political fervour. Until, by early March, just before the spring *rasputitsa*, I knew he would not stay with me for very much longer.

The evening before his departure I carefully laid out

his uniform, and in the morning I helped him dress into it once more. Then, watching him gently ride away, back into the conflict of civil war and the accursed Revolution, I bid farewell to my *Snyek Volk.

* Snow Wolf

The Fist
by G.R. Richards

The guys loomed large around the lockers when Deepak came out of the washroom. Between Walter and Rude Rudy's shoulders, he could just make out his door flung wide open. *Shit*. He had stuff in there he only wanted one person to see. Didn't they know the meaning of the word *privacy*? There was a reason lockers had locks.

'Hey, *Deep-packed*,' a voice called out. It was The Fist. He was standing behind the other two guys. When Walter and Rude Rudy shifted to the side, Deepak observed with horror what Fist had pulled from his locker. He was just plain mortified. There was no way to talk himself out of this one. 'What's this shit all about, eh? You planning on baking some brownies after work?'

The Fist. Believe it or not, they were tight. Deepak would never have imagined it when they first met. The guys all called him The Fist because he claimed to be a fighter. He *claimed* to be. The Fist talked a good talk. And when a big black guy talks, you listen. Once Deepak realised talk was all it was, he warmed up to Fist big-time. He figured anyone who worked so hard to maintain a hard outer shell had something vulnerable on the inside. Of course, he'd never admit that to Fist.

'Put it back,' Deepak begged. 'Please, before anyone else sees.'

At Fist's side, Walter shook his head. He looked over at Rudy to say, 'Well, I can't say I understand why any man would keep a slab of shortening in his locker.'

Walter. Everybody knew Walter was deaf in one ear. Some freak childhood accident, at least that was the rumour. He had a hearing aid, but didn't like to wear it in the warehouse. Too noisy. He got distortion, he said. Anyway, why waste batteries? Those things cost damn near a fortune. Walter was always hanging around The Fist. First off, they were cousins. Second off, he worried he'd be bullied by the other guys. Course, everyone loved Walter. Nobody would have laid a finger on him.

Rude Rudy was another story altogether. When Deepak first met the guy, he figured he'd be ... well ... *rude*. Crass. Tell dirty jokes, make suggestive comments. But that wasn't it. Rude Rudy was called Rude Rudy because he didn't have much to say. You could ask him a question and he'd give you a blank stare in return. Deepak asked Walter one time if maybe Rudy had a hearing impairment too. 'No,' Walter had told him. 'Rudy's just rude. He just don't care what you think of him.' Ever since, Deepak held Rudy in high esteem. He wished he could stop caring too.

As always, the tower of a man stared in silence. Deepak noticed his lips curling up at the sides. Rude Rudy knew why a person would have shortening in his locker, he just didn't want to explain.

'Cousin, you don't want to know what a man can get up to with a slab of shortening,' The Fist replied.

'I do now,' Walter said. 'You got me damn curious.'

Thank God for the boss! From the lunchroom door, he called, 'OK, enough chit-chat. Let's get back to work.'

The Fist slipped the box of shortening into the front pocket of his hooded sweater. As everyone else set off into the warehouse, the boss walked their way. Fist shut Deepak's locker door and leaned against it. 'To what do we owe the pleasure of your company?' Fist asked the boss.

'To the shit-load of cardboard boxes out by the compactor. They're full of fuckin' Styrofoam. You four want to deal with that?'

A smile broke across Rude Rudy's face. Walter spoke for all of them when he said, 'You got it.'

It was the easiest work in the warehouse. They must have weaselled their ways into the boss' good books. When they got to the compactors it looked like kids had been building box forts all around them. There was cardboard everywhere, piled way up high. Deepak started by dumping Styrofoam peanuts into clear bags. Packing could reuse them. The other guys broke down the empty boxes. Soon enough, Walter asked again, 'What's the story with the shortening? I can't get over that one.'

With a wide grin, The Fist pulled it from his pocket. 'Yeah, Deep,' he said, feigning innocence. 'Do tell. What's the story with the shortening?'

Deepak gritted his teeth. What did Fist expect him to say? He knew what it was for. Fishing the last few bits of Styrofoam from the bottom of a box, he mumbled, 'Leave me alone.'

'Are you sure you don't want me getting my hand all good and greasy?' Fist taunted, swaggering in Deepak's direction. He tossed the box of shortening up in the air, watched it flip, and caught it when it fell. 'Are you sure you don't want me shoving my fist up your ass?'

Walter gasped. 'What are you on about, Fist? Leave the Rudeness to Rudy. You just get your work done.'

Without lifting his animal gaze from his prey, Fist replied, 'Nothing to worry about, cousin. Deep's into it.'

He sliced along the tape line with his box cutter and tossed the limp sheet of cardboard to the floor. Sliding the blade in and out of casing, he looked Deepak up and down. *Was that supposed to be some kind of threat?*

'You like to get packed deep, don't you Deep-pack?' Fist sneered. Rudy picked up all the broken-down cardboard and tossed it in the compactor. All Deepak could concentrate on was the razor edge of the box-cutter's blade. In the close corner, Walter looked like he was going to shit himself. He jumped three feet in the air when Rudy pressed the big red button on the compactor. Even The Fist turned around when the big machine grunted, devouring a big pile of recyclables. They all stood still, mesmerised by the device until it squealed to a halt.

Walter was the first to speak. 'Why don't we all just break down these boxes? That's what the man's paying us for.'

'Deepak doesn't want to break boxes,' Fist mocked. He sauntered over to the first aid kit. With all the influenza concerns, management had installed wall-mounted hand sanitizing stations all over the place. Fist squirted some into his palm and sloshed it between his hands. 'All clean,' he said to Deepak. 'What's the story? You want me to deep-pack my fist in your ass?'

Deepak stepped around a huge bag of Styrofoam peanuts to get close to Fist. He choked back tears and hissed, 'You're humiliating me. Stop it. Just shut the fuck up, will you?'

The Fist's neat black eyebrows cocked in response. He thrived on impudence. Raising the box cutter to the shortening package, he slit the box open. Deepak stepped back, but slipped. Some luck, to fall on a bag of Styrofoam. He lay there, staring up at The Fist, the knife, and the shortening.

Gazing down at him, The Fist flipped the shortening into his palm and tossed the box to the floor. He placed the box cutter in one of the many pockets of his cargo pants before peeling waxy paper from the hunk of grease. 'You brought this shit to work for a reason,' The Fist said. He ran three dark fingers across the top of the shortening slab. The creamy stuff glistened as he rubbed it with his thumb.

'This is fuckin' crazy,' Deepak hissed. He tried to laugh, to downplay the threat, but he knew how insistent The Fist could be. As much as he didn't want to acknowledge the other guys' presence, he glanced at Walter in desperation.

'You think Walter's going to help you?' The Fist laughed. He slid his palm across the slab. When he closed his fist, globs of grease splattered out between his fingers. 'Walter ain't going to come to your rescue. Shit, he's your hear-no-evil monkey. Rudy there, he's your speak-no-evil monkey. And the rest of this warehouse? It's just one big-ass see-no-evil monkey. You got no chance, man. You just got to give in.'

Of course he was right. Sure, Deepak was scared shitless, but he was also so fuckin' horny he slid out of his jeans without waiting to be asked. From the corner, Walter gasped, 'What are you doing? Put your clothes on and get to work.'

The Fist only had to glance at him to get him to shut up. Walter was better than most at following instructions. He cowered in the corner while Deepak slid his jockeys down to his ankles. The plastic under his bare ass squealed. Without removing his safety boots, he kicked off his bottoms.

'Get breaking boxes,' The Fist instructed Walter.

'When Deep gets packed, we'll need that compactor to make some noise.'

Deepak's heart had never beaten so fast. He'd never seen his cock so hard. The Fist's hand gleamed a beautiful brown under the slick layer of shortening. His teeth sparkled when he smiled. Nobody else had lips like The Fist. If only he'd wrap them around his cock. Deepak was desperate for a blowjob.

'I'll do as you ask because you're family,' Walter said when he finally emerged from the corner. 'But I don't agree with what's going on here. We don't want no part in it, do we, Rudy?'

Rude Rudy stood tall. He made no response.

Deepak was still looking back at the guys when The Fist landed on the floor between his legs. He plunged his hand into the shortening and squeezed. His palm was covered in grease when he ran it along Deepak's straining shaft. 'There,' The Fist said. 'I want to see you jerk your fat cock while I finger-fuck your ass.'

His breaths were shallow as he replied, 'OK.' Course, it's not like anyone really had to beg him to jack it. He took his thick dick in hand and rubbed the slippery grease across his shaft. It felt so damn good he could have bust a nut. What would The Fist say if he did? He let go of his cock until the urge passed.

'I told you to hit your prick,' The Fist growled.

'Sorry,' Deepak sighed. He took it in hand and pumped. When The Fist traced his greased-up index finger around his asshole, he closed his eyes and tried to relax. Even one finger could be a task if he wasn't ready. He breathed deeply as The Fist ploughed him with the first finger. He could hear Walter gasping even as he sighed with pleasure.

The Fist offered some encouragement as his greasy

finger moved in circles. 'Deep, you got a tight little pussy-hole here, don't you?'

He pumped his cock slowly. He wanted to make his erection last as long as possible. 'I'm sorry,' he said. 'I know it's tight.'

'Hey, don't *sorry* me,' The Fist laughed. 'You're the one who's going to get a fist all up in there.' He grabbed hold of Deepak's thigh as he shoved a second finger inside.

Inhaling sharply, Deepak stroked his dick from base to tip. If he were just pounding one out, he'd go straight at his cockhead until it sprayed jizz. But he wanted to make this one last. For The Fist.

Three fingers. 'Tight fuckin' fit,' The Fist said. Like he knew the half of it. Three fingers to the knuckles. Deepak tugged his meat while The Fist plunged inside. Firm, greasy fingers fucked him good.

'Time for more shortening,' Fist said, plunging his hand into the destroyed slab. He knew what would come next. Fist would skip from three to five. The pinky was a stupid finger. It didn't deserve time wasted on it. He'd fold the pinky in with the other three, then press his thumb flat against his palm. It wasn't really a fist at all. It was more like a bulb. Getting fisted wasn't like getting punched. It was more like getting fed full-up. With his greased hand, The Fist prepared to nourish him.

When those slippery fingers set against Deepak's hole, he could feel his assring expanding like an infinite elastic. It kept getting looser to let The Fist in. Not all at once. It wasn't like tight to slack in six seconds. Took time. Took breathing. Took a kind of give and take. Fist knew not to rush. Rush it, and it's all over. You're bleeding, you're in pain, and you hate the guy who did it to you. Take your time, and it feels better than any damn thing you've ever done in your life. The Fist took his time.

Concentrating on The Fist's focused expression, Deepak beat his rod. As he pulled on it, slick fingers eased their way through the welcoming ring of his asshole. God damn it, Fist was hot. He didn't think his ecstasy could reach greater heights until heavy footsteps resounded behind him. *Shit! The boss was coming!* His ass got so tight it trapped Fist's fingertips in place. But when he instinctively turned his head to see, it wasn't the boss at all. Rude Rudy approached as Walter turned a blind eye, slicing through boxes over by the compactor.

Rudy unlatched his overalls. He didn't seem to notice as they fell to the floor. His sleeveless top was short enough for Deepak to get a good look at his commando cock before it lodged itself down his throat. He choked as Rudy knelt on the bag of Styrofoam peanuts, one knee on either side of his head. But his main concern wasn't for himself. How would The Fist feel about him sucking another guy's cock?

When Rude Rudy threw himself forward and swallowed Deepak's wood, he immediately stopped sputtering. He didn't mind so much deep-throating a guy who returned the favour. Fist laughed in the background. *Thank God he wasn't mad!* Last think Deepak wanted to do was inadvertently piss off the guy with four fingers in his ass.

He wouldn't have expected Rude Rudy to be a pro cocksucker, but he sure as shit was. The heavy aroma of sweaty man-ass took over Deepak's senses as soft lips encircled his tip. When a wicked tongue slid down his shaft, he gasped out loud. He tried to keep quiet, but no use. It all felt too damn good.

'Turn on the compactor,' The Fist said to Walter. 'When this kid blows, it's going to be epic.'

Walter grumbled, but that was only audible until he followed instructions and turned on the machine. It made the floor tremble. It devoured cardboard while he devoured Rudy and Rudy devoured him. Reaching under his T-shirt, Deepak pinched his nipples. *God, that felt awesome!* His ass must have swallowed an inch of Fist's hand in response. There was so damn much going on he could hardly keep track of it all.

When he opened his eyes, it was Rude Rudy's toned body he saw above him. Even with the compactor humming in the background, he could still hear the man groaning as he ate his hard meat. The plastic bag they were on must have sprung a leak, because every so often a Styrofoam peanut would fly up in the air and flutter back down.

His ass got filled in the midst of all this. Deepak had little sense of *it's in* or *it's not in*. Fisting was relative. It was all the same sensation, just in varying degrees. His hole felt full and slick. The more Fist's hand entered him, the more packed he felt. He had no sense of whether Fist was in his ass up to the knuckles or whether he was farther along than that.

In the background, the compactor churned to a halt. He could hear Walter working his ass off to get more boxes broken down. Poor guy. Left to work all on his own while the others sucked and fist-fucked. Deepak opened his legs and dug his feet into the ground while Fist spread even more grease around. He was getting in there deep. He knew exactly what Fist was about to say when he opened his mouth. 'You feeling Deep-packed yet?'

Deepak responded yes, though with a mouth full of cock, his answer was completely garbled. He'd never felt so full in his life. His asshole tried its damnedest to close, but of course there was a wrist in the way. He could feel

53

Rude Rudy laughing as he sucked like a banshee. When he pinched his own little nipples, all the combined pleasures overwhelmed him. Even with The Fist's hand up his ass, he thrust up into Rudy's throat. Rudy thrust down into his. They were making some serious noise. Enough that The Fist said, 'Walter, turn that fucking thing back on.'

The compactor grunted louder than even the three of them could manage. Deepak was pretty sure he and Rudy came together, filling each other's mouths with hot come simultaneously. He couldn't stop shaking, even as Rudy pressed up and away from him. Styrofoam peanuts went flying into the air. His thighs trembled. It didn't matter that Rude Rudy's silent mouth was gone. Come still pumped from his cockhead, warming his skin.

Without all the distraction of sucking cock, Deepak clearly felt The Fist's fingers opening slightly and closing back up against the walls of his ass. He didn't seem at all upset about Rude Rudy's involvement. In fact, The Fist watched in seeming amazement as the strong silent man pulled up his overalls and sauntered over to the gap in boxes. He'd keep a lookout for the boss while The Fist turned his hand in slow pivots. Getting out was a lot like getting in. Took time.

'I don't believe this,' Walter muttered in the background. He was the only one still dumping Styrofoam and breaking down boxes. 'I do not believe what I see.'

Gazing into The Fist's hard gaze, Deepak fought back tears. 'I don't believe it either,' he said. 'Doing this to my body right here in the warehouse, in front of your cousin and Rudy? This is humiliating.'

'Humiliating?' The Fist chuckled. When he turned his hand side to side, Deepak squeezed his hard titties

54

underneath his T-shirt. That never failed. His assring loosened for The Fist. 'You can't fool me. You love getting packed deep.' His hand felt huge as it emerged from his ass.

Deepak tried not to push, but his body's instinct was to expel. 'Why are you doing this to me?'

'Because you want it,' The Fist said. 'That's why you brought this grease to work.' As his knuckles began their brave escape, the pressure on his assring mounted. It started with a whimper, but soon Deepak couldn't conceal his pleasure-pained cries.

'Turn on the compactor,' Fist hissed at Walter. He wasted no time.

As the compactor rumbled to a start, Deepak pinched his nipples. He moaned at the huge sensation in his hole, but the machine covered his tracks.

'You wanted me to shove my whole hand in your ass,' The Fist accused. Deepak could only just hear him over the compactor's rumble. The sneer on his lips made him feel small. He was a tiny, tight little hole and The Fist was mammoth. 'Admit it. You wanted this.'

'You're humiliating me,' Deepak repeated.

The Fist cocked his eyebrows. His hand retreated.

A wild shriek exploded from Deepak as a set of knuckles raged through his assring. *Thank God for the damn compactor!* He couldn't explain the tears in his eyes as The Fist rested four fingers just inside his hole. It felt so damn good to be full. Now he was open, but there was nothing inside him. Not really.

The Fist pulled out his fingers and stared Deepak straight in the face. His legs were splayed wide open, his spent cock resting on his pelvis, and his asshole taking its time to close up shop. The compactor roared in the background.

'I've never been so humiliated. Not in my whole life,' Deepak said. He was so exhausted he couldn't even smile.

The Fist had no trouble smiling. A grin wide as daybreak broke across his lips as he leaned up close. 'I thought you'd like that.'

The compactor's wild reverberations made it impossible to think of something original to say. But if he couldn't be original, at least he could be heartfelt. There was no way Walter or Rude Rudy could hear, with that machine going strong, so Deepak sighed, 'That was the best gift I've ever gotten.'

The Fist shrugged like it wasn't a big deal. As the compactor squealed to a standstill, he whispered, 'Happy anniversary.'

Wired
by Landon Dixon

I got a sense this was going to be one of my more interesting jobs when I saw Dan and Elliot fucking in the basement.

I'd gone down there, innocently enough, to get to the main electrical box and trip a few breakers. The guys had hired me to do a total rewire of their upstairs. And now I was getting more than a little wired myself – watching the two men get a big charge out of each other.

My work boots on the wooden stairs didn't give me away, because the two lovers had classic Queen blaring out of a battery-powered ghetto blaster. Dan had Elliot flat on his back on the pool table at the far end of the rec room, vigorously slamming his cock into the writhing guy's asshole as Freddy Merc hit all the right high notes.

I thought about retracing my steps backwards up the stairs, discreetly waiting for the horndogs to finish what they'd started. Which judging from the sweat shining on Dan's rocking back and bucking butt cheeks, the excited grunting and groaning of the shunted Elliot sounding even over the rollicking guitar licks, wasn't too far in the offing.

But as I squatted down on the stairs and clenched the wooden slats of the railing, watching Dan's trim, tanned hips churning, Elliot's pale, muscular legs bouncing off the guy's thin shoulders, Elliot flinging his head from side-to-side and pinching and pulling on his nipples, I thought, Right here is where I want to be – taking a break and taking in the electric show these livewires are putting on. So, I maintained my position, the 15 hour quote I'd given the guys going into overtime.

Dan was a long, lean, blond drink of quenching water, with a ready smile and an all-over tan that packed even more wattage than his teeth. He liked to dress in short-shorts and a muscle shirt when he was hanging around the house. Although right now, the shorts were down around his slim ankles and the muscle shirt off his slender torso and strewn on the carpeted floor.

His bare, brown ass was really something to behold, the taut cheeks deliciously clenching and unclenching with every hard thrust of his hips. The lean muscles on his back tightening and jumping as he clutched Elliot's legs, banged the guy's body back and forth on the plastic-covered pool table. From my backside side angle, I couldn't see Dan's cock gloriously stretching his buddy's asshole, but I could well imagine the depths that dick was hitting, based on the way his shorts bulged whenever I'd seen him.

Elliot was smaller, but thicker, a dark-haired, muscular guy with fair skin and plush red lips, and clear blue eyes that took your breath away. I could see most of his bare upper body laid out on that pool table, from around Dan's hinging frame. And what I saw was as lip-smacking and mouth-watering as the blond's rear view: pink, proudly-jutting nipples, a smooth, muscle-plated chest gleaming ivory under the bright lights. His mouth was open and eyes closed, rugged hands on his chest, thick fingers rolling those rigid nipples, chiselled body getting delightfully dong-blasted to and fro.

My bent legs trembled as bad as Dan's, as I watched the erotic pair blow their sexual fuses, my sweaty hands staining the varnished wood, almost squeezing the slats to sawdust. My cock was a live, coursing cable in my jeans, packed at an awkward angle and yearning to be unravelled.

The thumping 70s music reached a crescendo. And so did Dan, the guy pistoning his hips in a frenzy, surging cock into Elliot's anus. I heard the sweet, lusty smack of corded thighs against tight buttocks, even above Freddy's impassioned wailing – beating faster and faster.

'Oh, God! I'm coming!' the fair-haired top hollered, his sweat-sheened body jerking, shaking out of control. He shot up onto his tiptoes, wildly pumping, blasting sizzling jizz into Elliot's blown-open ass.

And Elliot's eyes shot open, as he felt the scalding splash of semen against his bowels. 'Come in my ass, you fucking bastard!' he yelled, egging the frantically thrusting guy on. 'Fucking fill me to the rim with your hot come!'

Dan threw back his head and howled as loud and long as the lead singer of Queen, emptying his balls into his buddy, his sweat-drenched, sun kissed body vibrating like the rock n' roll rocked basement walls.

I counted his spasms, shaking my head in amazement when the beautiful butt-fucker hit double digits. He must've been spilling out of Elliot's ass as he was gushing in, obviously saving up for some time for this special occasion.

My own cock was painfully erect in the crumpled crotch of my jeans, my balls boiling towards overload. I had to hastily shift position to ease the pressure, because the man show was far from over.

Finally finished juicing his lover's sexual core, the

luscious blond beanpole popped out of Elliot's ass and dropped to his knees on the carpet. While Elliot popped up on the pool table and butt-crawled to the edge. So that in one swift, oiled motion, Dan was squatting between Elliot's legs, Elliot's cock in his mouth.

The blond's head bobbed back and forth in Elliot's crotch, his long fingers digging into the man's meaty, splayed thighs. The muscle stud tilting his head back with joy and digging his own fingers into his buddy's hair, taking his cocksucking like a man.

I got a brief glimpse of Elliot's spit-shone glory, when Dan dropped his head down to suck on the guy's balls. The muscleman was packing some serious pipe, his pink, purple-headed, vein-popped dong poling out eight inches or more; straight and thick and cut and twitching with every tug of Dan's lips on his sack.

My mouth hung open with hunger at the awesome display of all that succulent meat, my whole body shaking with second-hand lust. Dan replaced his mouth with his hand on the hung-man's balls and licked up and down the groaning guy's shaft, painting Elliot's prong ten shades of sensual.

And Elliot was obviously as keyed up from the butt-blasting he'd just taken as I was. Because Dan had only got five or six good tongue lashes in, from dark-furred base to bloated hood, when Elliot grunted loud and imperative and clawed at the charming cock-teaser's thatch, heated come leaping out the mushroomed tip of his slickened prick. A gushing fountain of pearly-white semen rained down on lucky Dan's upturned face and outthrust tongue.

I couldn't take it any more; the music and masculine mayhem making my cock pulsate with pre-come. I just made it to the main floor toilet in time, an electric current of jism shooting out of my sparking cock, ecstasy arcing all through my body and soul.

I was hunched over by the floorboards in the upstairs master bedroom the next morning when I heard someone snarl, 'I saw you watching us the other day!'

I twisted my head around, stared at Elliot filling the doorway with his rugged frame. 'Huh? What? I d-don't know what you're ...'

'Bullshit!' He strode into the bedroom, boxing me into the corner.

I dropped the wire I'd been threading through and scrambled to my feet. The angry guy was wearing a thin blue bathrobe, his muscles bulging the seams, his feet bare, his handsome face hard and uncompromising. I spluttered, 'No ... I mean ...'

'You were on the stairs watching me and Dan yesterday afternoon!' he retorted, getting right up into my chest and poking me a solid one with a rigid forefinger. 'Fucking pervert!'

He was a good four inches shorter than me and 20 or 30 pounds lighter. But he was built. Oh, how he was built.

'No – no! I was, uh, working – all the time,' I protested, trying to avoid the hypnotic glare of his shining blue eyes.

'Yeah, right!'

He grabbed my arms and spun me around, shoved me backwards. I tumbled onto the big, four-poster bed.

Just as Dan rushed in, his long, lithe legs spilling out of a pair of tight white shorts, bright red muscle shirt hanging off his long, burnished torso. 'Hey, what's going on in here!?' he asked.

Elliot ignored him, jumping on top of me on the bed, straddling my chest and pinning me down. Dan ran

61

forward and seized the guy around the shoulders and tried to pull him off. But the only thing that came off was Elliot's bathrobe, slipping down his cinder block shoulders. He angrily un-sashed it and flung it aside, leaving him utterly naked on top of me, his sledge of a cock carving out a warm burrow in my chest, barely a foot from my open mouth.

I stared up at the guy, down at his dong, too surprised and impressed to fight back. Too admiring of his smooth, ripped physique and the firm press of his buttocks on my chest, that club of a cock so close, to offer anything but passive resistance.

'That's quite enough, Elliot!' Dan huffed, standing next to the bed with his hands on his hips.

'Like hell it is!' the tough boy gritted. 'I'm gonna teach this peeping Tim a lesson.'

My first name's Tim, so it made sense.

'Hey, I didn't mean to ...' I began. And was cut off again.

By Elliot ordering Dan, 'Get some of that wire off the floor!' He turned his head back to look down at me again, a hard grin on his face. 'We're gonna teach this perv a lesson about getting off on others.'

I swallowed my Adam's apple and part of my tongue, as Dan now quickly obliged his studly lover, trimming off strands of red and black-jacketed wire from the spools I'd left lying around on the floor. Then he tied my ankles and wrists to the bedposts with the insulated wire, while Elliot kept me pinned down on the bed, his hammer growing longer, larger, heavier on my heaving chest.

And once I was firmly trussed up, Elliot slid down my trembling body so that he was straddling my legs. Looking me in the gaping eyes, he unbuckled my belt and unzipped my pants, yanked my jeans and Jockeys down in

one fell swoop. My cock sprung out into the open –
achingly, embarrassingly hard.

Now smiling a whole lot less maliciously and a lot
more mischievously – I thought, and hoped – Elliot
regarded my shameful display and said, 'What'd I tell you
– a fucking pervert! Hand me a strip of that red wire,
Dan.'

Blondie cut off a length, handed it to his buddy. And,
still grinning, my dark and dangerous tormentor wound
the strand around and around the ginger-furred base of my
cock, the remainder around my balls. He tied my genitals
up and together so that I stood tall and bloated, my
strangled, swollen cock making an outrageously obscene
gesture at the gloating men.

I grinned sheepishly. Then I noticed that Dan had
somehow become as nude as his sexy companion, the
blond crowding close to the head of the bed, his smooth,
bronze, arrow-straight erection staring me right in the
mouth.

'You should've kept your eyes on your work, Mr
Bacco,' he commented, shaking his finger and cock at me.

At that same instant I felt a wet, wonderful heat
suddenly envelop my ballooned-up cap – Elliot's red lips,
engulfing my up-thrust hood and descending my towering
shaft. 'Sweet Jesus!' I yelped, watching the guy slowly,
sensuously take almost my entire wound-up pole into his
warm, moist mouth.

I strained against my bindings, but couldn't break free,
feeling and not feeling the man's soft lips and cushioning
tongue on my wrangled prick. The sweet, sensitive
sucking pressure as he bobbed his head up and down. It
was erotic torture of the most exquisitely excruciating
kind, and I twisted my head around on the pillows,
fighting to feel more.

Dan gave me something more to feel, clamping a pair of electrical pincers to my engorged nipples, and tweaking. I arched my body, my cock into Elliot's throat, like I'd been electrocuted. And Dan stepped up and partially filled the screaming void in my anguished sexual soul, by sticking his cock into my open mouth.

I latched my slavering lips onto the man's meaty head and frantically sucked, chewed, Elliot playing a strange, savage tune on my roped skin-flute. Dan fed me more and more of his cock, which I gratefully gulped down. His gorgeous member was rock-hard yet smooth as silk, gliding into my greedy mouth and up against the back of my throat. He sifted his fingers into my red hair and really grabbed hold, churning his prick back and forth in my mouth.

I urgently sucked on the heated, sweat-scented meat, gasping for air through my nose, straining my eyes to watch Elliot pull on my own cock with his sensual lips and mouth. He bit into my hood, swirled his thick, wet tongue all around my cockhead, licked up and down my throbbing shaft. As I desperately struggled to feel the full force of it – and couldn't, tied off at the balls.

'Lube me, sweet cheeks,' the dark-haired cocksucker suddenly said to his mouth-fucking companion, popping his head up from my groin.

Dan plucked a tube of lube off the nightstand and tossed it to Elliot, not breaking the beat in my mouth. Elliot greased my prick with the love oil, then the crack of his ass. And I held my breath – choking on Dan's surging cock – as Elliot squatted over my stake. Then slowly lowered himself down, and in, filling his chute to bursting with my swelled-up cock: until his clenched cheeks touched down on my quivering thighs.

He held the awesome position for a moment – my cock

buried to the balls in his ass – all three of us and the bed shaking now. Then he started bouncing up and down, fucking himself on my prong.

I blew snot out my billowing nostrils like an oxygen-starved whale breaking the surface, revelling in the agonisingly muted sensations of the wicked heat and tightness of the guy's chute. Dan pumped faster, pistoning cock between my lips, bouncing hood off the back of my throat. The bedposts rattling, bed jumping.

Every fibre of my being screamed for sexual release. I was bathed in sweat, flushed with heat, my eyes bugging out and body flopping around like the wires that bound me were bare and alive. But there was just no way I could get off on the wild scene; I was just tied up too tight at all my appendages.

My two playful antagonists were getting off, though, Dan gripping my head and power-shafting my mouth like he'd been shafting Elliot's ass the previous day; Elliot gripping my chest with one hand and bounding his butt up and down on my prick, ardently fisting his own flapping member with his other hand.

'Oh, God, here it comes!' Dan cried, flooding my mouth with hot, salty spunk; dousing my throat with burst after fiery burst, which I excitedly swallowed.

'Fuck, yeah! Yeah!' Elliot bellowed, trembling on the end of my cock and jerking long ropes of white-hot semen out of his prick, striping my face and chest and stomach.

Dan shuddered and shot his load, emptying his shaven sack inside of me, his cock jumping in my mouth. As Elliot came all over me, thumping up and down on top of me, burying my cock to his bowels as he blew out his balls on my chest.

And then finally, at last, it was my turn to howl with triumphal ecstasy. When Dan unplugged his cock and

Elliot mine and the two men unleashed me.

They unwrapped my cock and balls which instantly regained circulation and flooded with butter, jizz blasting out of my slit and showering my face and torso. Again and again and again. Coming hands-free and harder and longer than I'd ever come before.

That fifteen-hour rewiring job turned into an exhausting, exhilarating two-week marathon engagement that I never wanted to end.

But with a bank account as drained as my body, unfortunately, I was eventually forced to move on.

Unleashing a Demon
by Eva Hore

Football season was finally over. We'd been to Europe for our end-of-year footy trip and still had a week left. On returning to Melbourne, Brad and I had decided to spend a few more days together. His parents had a holiday house down at Torquay and I heard there was a nudist beach hidden amongst the coastline. Brad had never been to one. I said we should check it out.

'Come on, let's go,' Brad said, jumping out of the car before I'd even parked.

'I'm not sure I want to now.'

'Why?'

'It's just not my thing,' I lied.

I was nervous and excited at the prospect of spending time being naked, with Brad, but I wasn't quite sure how to go about it, how to act in front of him once we'd stripped off. I was nervous about how he'd react to me if I came on to him.

'Don't be a dickhead, come on,' Brad said.

I locked the car.

We strolled along the water's edge; our sunglasses still on so we could have a *perv*. There weren't many people out, a few old women with droopy tits and a couple of old guys with saggy testicles. They nodded hello. We acknowledged them and kept on walking.

We found a semi-secluded spot out of view of the oldies. Brad stripped right off, his fantastic body rippling with muscles. He stood and stretched. His cock, like a thick cobra, flopped from side to side as the sun kissed his naked flesh.

Me, I stripped off too, but more slowly. I was embarrassed as I'd cracked half a fat. Seeing Brad naked always did that to me. The guy was fucking gorgeous. We'd know each other for years, having gone to the same schools, but since we'd joined the football team, we'd gotten close, real close. Now we were too close. Naked and close.

Me, I knew I was gay, but Brad, well I didn't think he knew what he wanted. Whenever the team went out to the pub, it was usually Brad and I who sat back and watched, commenting on all the others, neither of us even attempting to pick up girls. I was happy to wait for him to realise what he was missing, and I was hoping it would be soon that he'd realise he was missing me. Being so close to him made it hard for me, real hard.

'Feels good, doesn't it?' he said, lying back against the sand, his elbows digging in, his thighs open to the sun as his cock lay thick on the inside of his thigh.

'Yeah, it's great. Glad you made me come.' I laughed, more comfortable now that he seemed so relaxed.

It felt fucking fantastic. The sun bore down on me, over my balls and cock, heating me up, making me hotter and hotter as I snuck longing looks at Brad from behind my sunglasses. More comfortable now I could see his cock. He was clearly enjoying himself. I licked my lips as I gazed down at his cock. It had grown and I wondered how it would taste to lick his knob, to suck his shaft deep into my throat.

'Check out this guy,' Brad whispered, as a young

Italian stud strode past.

The guy was dark all over, with a thick black patch of pubic hair covering most of his abdomen and lower regions. His cock hung like a stallion's, over his huge balls. It preceded him as he walked.

'Show off,' I laughed.

'Did you see the size of it?'

Brad was clearly impressed.

'Hmm,' I muttered, eyeing the guy's arse as he walked off. 'His isn't much bigger than ours.'

'You've got to be kidding,' he said, leaning over to look down at mine. 'Hey, I never realised how big you were, man.'

I tried to cover up but he slapped my hand away.

'Don't be embarrassed, man,' he said. 'Shit, if mine was that big, I'd be letting everyone see.'

I jumped up and ran down to the water's edge. I could barely contain my excitement. My cock was throbbing. Icy cold water splashed against it immediately causing it to shrink down to a more acceptable size. Looking over my shoulder, I saw Brad not far behind me. I dived into a wave and began to swim, enjoying the feel of the water as it glided against me, against my naked flesh.

Brad caught up and we swam for a while before body surfing back in. The last wave knocked me off balance and as I tried to stand, the receding wave had me toppling over. Laughing, Brad kicked water at me and ran back to our towels. He flopped on top of his, while I trudged up behind him.

The old couple was in the process of packing up. The rest of the beach was empty from what I could see.

'That felt great,' Brad said, watching me as I approached.

'Didn't it, though,' I said, noting how Brad's eyes

were roaming over my torso before settling on my cock.

'I never realised what a great cock you've got there,' he said.

I flopped on my towel; droplets of water covered my skin. His eyes were still on me, boring into my cock like a red hot rod, igniting a fire in me that needed to flare, grow and rage out of control.

'What are you talking about? We're about the same size,' I insisted.

He looked from his to mine and the more he looked the more I grew.

'Bullshit,' he said, his fingers stretching out to measure himself before coming back to me.

'I just want to compare,' he said, eyeing me to gauge my reaction as he carefully put his hand down near me.

Brad's eyes widened as he studied me. His fingers were nearly touching me, so I concentrated as much as possible to make it lift and throb, willing it to grow before his very eyes. I said nothing. I just lay there with my hands behind my head, my cock pulsating visibly as Brad continued to stare. His fingers edged closer. He grazed the side of my knob but said nothing. Neither did I.

Brad leaned back on his towel and looked out to sea. I knew there was no one about. The Italian had disappeared. The area we were in hid us from prying eyes. The old couple were beginning to move off so it was going to be just me and him. Brad picked up suntan lotion and began to apply it over his torso before lavishing his groin, thighs and legs. His body shone, slick with oil. It took all my willpower not to touch him, not to make a move on him. And all the while my cock continued to grow.

'Want me to put some lotion on you?' he asked.

'Sure,' I said.

I watched him lick his lips as his palms spread the lotion over my torso. As he neared my belly button, he squeezed some more on my skin and then quickly rubbed it in, going further and further towards my cock. His fingers slipped through my pubic hair. I held my breath as his fingers dipped down into my groin, over my balls before coming up the base of my shaft. Then, his hand lightly ran up my cock, his fingers slipping up and down before gliding over my knob as sticky pre-come touched his fingers. Still I said nothing, content to let things take their own course. Without looking at me, his fingers trailed over the knob, around the underside of skin and then slowly down the shaft and then back up again, only barely touching me.

'Man, you've got the biggest cock I've ever seen,' he said.

I breathed a sigh of relief and my cock responded by becoming more rigid, pleased with all this attention. Finally, I was getting what I'd been wanting for such a long time. Finally Brad.

'Hold it!' I whispered.

'What?'

'Grab hold of it,' I said, in a firm voice.

He looked to me, then down at my cock and then back to me. I nodded.

'Do it, please.'

Cautiously, his hand closed around the shaft. It was like lightning soaring through me. My cock throbbed painfully under his grip. I wanted him to pull at it, to jerk me off, to suck me into his mouth.

'Oh, man, that feels good,' he said.

'Hmm, real good,' I whispered back encouragingly.

'I've … I've never done this before,' he said, avoiding eye contact.

'That's OK,' I chuckled. 'I have.'

He relaxed and began to stroke it, gently at first and then more firmly. I closed my eyes as his grip tightened and he slowly pumped up and down before his rhythm became bolder, more daring. I was forced to ask him to slow down.

'Take it easy,' I whispered. 'Nice and gentle, like this.'

I reached for him.

'Hey,' someone shouted. 'What are you guys doing?'

It was the old couple. I thought they'd left. Fuck! The guy was shaking his finger at us. Brad pulled away. His face reddened. I had been just about ready to blow. When the couple were out of sight, I lunged for him. I grabbed at his shaft, pumping up and down, enjoying listening to him moan as he fell back onto the towel. His cock thickened again, the skin stretching tight against his knobby veins. My hand moved further downwards to cup his balls. They were tight and hot. I leaned forward and covered his knob with my mouth. He pulled back a fraction and then relaxed. Brad liked it. I ran my tongue over the top, slathering it with saliva. His hand came down on my head, pushing me further down on him until I swallowed his shaft.

'Oh God,' he whispered.

Fuck, he was rock hard. I sucked him deep inside my mouth, loving the feel of him, loving the feel of his cock as the blood gushed and coursed through him. His moaning became louder, more ardent, his knob swelling. I knew it wouldn't be long before he came.

'Bring … bring your cock up here,' he said, slapping my back.

I maneuvered around without taking my mouth off him, until I straddled his head. His fist closed around me. He began to lick my knob, cautiously at first, but before

72

long, he was slathering me with his saliva. Then he sucked me deep into his throat, the two of us not caring at this stage if anyone stumbled upon us. Fuck old couples. It took only minutes for us to come. I sucked hungrily, gobbling down his spunk as he devoured mine.

I collapsed on him, sand sticking to my sweaty skin. The combination of the sun and the aftermath of what had just happened had my head spinning.

'Fuck,' he said.

'Hmm,' I muttered.

We lay there like that for a while, each of us with our own thoughts. Then we ran to the water again, wrestling with each other as the waves knocked us about. Swimming further out, we trod water as we kissed passionately, our tongues seeking out each others, desperate to explore the recesses.

Later, as the sun began to set, we lay on our towels and Brad's fingers ran along my flesh. I opened my legs, making it easier for him. His finger wiggled around my hairy crack before coming to rest on my puckered hole. This was going better than I thought. This was closer to Brad than I had ever imagined possible. His mouth descended over my cock, the warmth from his mouth heating me up much more than the sun could ever have.

'Hmm,' he mumbled, swallowing me up further as his finger probed me.

I looked down as my cock disappeared into his mouth, the knob hitting the back of his throat and stroked his hair.

'Fuck, it's big,' he mumbled.

Running my fingers through his hair, I held onto his head and pushed my cock in deeper. He gagged for a second, pulling back a bit and then he continued to suck. I could feel my passion rising and yanked him back by the hair.

73

'I want to fuck you,' he said.

'Good,' I laughed.

'Roll over on your side,' he demanded.

I rolled. His tongue rimmed my hole, flickering about crazily as he slathered it with saliva. I could sense his urgency, his need. Before long his knob was gently probing me, trying desperately to inch its way in. I relaxed and after a moment's hesitation, he slipped in.

At first he pushed in slowly, easing in and out, wanting not to hurt me, but I pushed back, egging him on, desperate for a good fucking. He started to thrust into me, pounding my arse as though he'd been doing it for years.

'Up on all fours,' he ordered.

I loved him being assertive, taking the initiative. This was a new Brad, a Brad out of control. He knelt in behind me, pulled my arse cheeks apart and dove right in. His fingers gripped my flesh as he slammed into me. Then he was slapping at my thighs, riding me hard before exploding inside me.

I fell to the ground as he pulled away. But I was hungry for him. He was on his back, breathing hard, his cock flaccid now, lying on his thigh. I flew down to his cock. Sucked him deep into the back of my throat building up my saliva so he slid in and out rhythmically. His limp and exhausted cock began to swell in my mouth.

'Oh, yeah. Suck my dick, man.'

I did for a while, but what I really wanted to do was fuck his arse too. Leaving his cock, I made my way down to the base of his shaft while my fingers played with his balls. Sucking his hairy balls into my mouth, my fingers continued further towards the crack of his arse where I found *his* puckered hole. I tickled the skin there and felt his hand on my head pushing me further down towards his hole. I didn't need anymore encouragement. Brad was ready.

Lying between his open thighs I lifted a leg and threw it over so he lay more on his side. Opening up his arse cheeks, I licked his crack lovingly, up and down before resting on his hole. With my tongue trying to find its way in, I gave him a good rimming, lubing him up for what soon would be his first time I hoped. His first gay fuck. I manoeuvred my way behind him so I was spooning him, my cock probing his arse.

'Hey, man,' he said nervously. 'I don't think that fucker's going to fit. It's too fucking big.'

'Oh, it will fit all right,' I said.

'Be gentle with me then.'

My cock slid between his legs nudging up against his balls while my hand slid over his hip and down into his groin. His cock was rock hard now. I held onto it, pumping it while my cock continued to rub up against him.His hand came down to cover mine and I left him to wank himself while I grabbed my own cock and with my other hand pried open his arse cheeks.

'Come on,' I whispered. 'Let me in, Brad.'

I continued to nudge his opening. He pushed back into me, grinding his arse into my groin.

'Easy, easy,' he said, while I was trying to inch it in.

'Oh God, you're so fucking tight.'

Maybe too tight. I didn't want his first time to be too painful. I needed him to relax, let go of his muscles and perhaps his apprehension. I pushed gently, probing further as I pulled his cheeks apart and the knob began to slip in.

'Oh fuck,' he moaned and I felt him tense.

'Relax,' I said.

'It's too big, man. It's too fucking big.'

'Just relax.'

With my knob barely in, my hand snaked under and

75

weighed his balls, squeezing them gently as he played with his cock.

'I don't want to hurt you,' I said.

'You won't,' he conceded. 'Just give it to me.'

'You sure?' I said.

'Real sure,' he urged.

Grabbing hold of his hips, I manoeuvred him around until he was up on all fours. With him in this position, I was able to grab hold of his hips and guide my cock gently inside. Slowly I built up the pressure, inching in. I could feel some resistance and pulled back.

He flung his head up.

'Keep going, but just take it easy.'

I pushed in further, slowly and carefully. I slapped at his thigh, hard.

'Oh shit,' he moaned. 'I think it's too fucking big.'

Inching it in further, he cried out with pain. I pulled back a bit, eased back in, just getting him used to the size, just wanting him to relax and not tense up. I wanted, needed his arse. Brad's arse. I slapped his thigh again, then his cheek. He liked it. Liked a bit of a spanking, so I slapped his cheeks, taking his mind off my cock. I felt him let go, relax further so I slipped in further. He was tight, real tight. But I eased in and out gently, giving him the occasional slap as he moaned with pleasure.

'Oh, yeah. That's great,' he said.

I sensed he was just trying to say the right thing. I knew this was hurting. I tried to pick up the tempo. He screamed with pain as I inched in further him. His hole needed stretching if I was ever going to fit my full cock inside him. Sweat was pouring off me and I watched it drip onto his back. My knees hurt, the pressure from the sand digging in. I pulled my cock out and shook it against his hole. Giving it a good pull, I wanked off with the tip of my cock pushing back against his hole.

'Oh God, I'm coming,' he cried out, his body slick with sweat.

'Me too,' I said, giving my cock one last pull so I could spray a load all over his back.

I collapsed on top of him. We stayed like that for a few moments each of us trying to catch our breath, before falling onto the sand.

'You OK?' I said.

'God, that was great,' he said.

It was dusk. The sun setting on the sea left a pink hue on the horizon. I smiled to myself, pleased with how the day had gone; pleased I'd been right about Brad. I was sated and exhausted.

'But I'm still feeling horny,' he said.

His fingers tweaked a nipple, pulling at it hard before he sucked it into his mouth to tug at it with his teeth.

'Hey,' I complained.

'You'd better roll over and get up on all fours,' he said.

'You serious?' I asked.

'You'd better believe it,' he chuckled. 'You hurt me, I hurt you.'

I'd unleashed a demon; an insatiable demon. It's been fun trying to tame him ever since.

The Running Man
by Jade Taylor

When the running gets too hard I always think about what I'm running back to.

Who I'm running back to.

He's not my lover, waiting in bed for my return, sleepy eyed and waking horny, wondering how long I'll be. He's not my friend, ready to meet me for morning coffee, to ask how far I've run today. He's not even a colleague, someone I get to see every day with a brisk *hello, how are you?* that's never truly answered.

But he's my neighbour.

It isn't enough, shouldn't be enough, that when I push my body too hard, that when I run to the limits of my exhaustion, the thought of him should still make me run back home.

But somehow it is.

I'm rangy, not prone to putting weight on, and though I have a worrying fondness for Ben & Jerry's ice cream, I eat well and healthily. But I'm prone to loneliness in this new city of mine, to worrying, over-thinking things rather than acting impulsively, and the running helps me vent some steam.

It also stops me thinking about how long it is since I got laid.

Though running back, thinking about my neighbour, does not.

He's tall and dark, with one of those cheeky smiles that seem to imply he's constantly thinking lascivious thoughts. I've only ever seen him in smart suits, but once, when he had his sleeves rolled up, I saw the edge of a tattoo peeking through, that made me want to get closer, to explore his body more thoroughly.

He has broad shoulders, and though I've never seen him in jeans, it would be a dream come true, his tight little ass obvious despite his well cut trousers.

He has big blue eyes, made even more striking by his dark hair and skin, and eyelashes that go on for ever.

He's out, but not flamboyant, and I can't help but admire the easy way he handles his sexuality as if it were part of him that should be as easily accepted as the colour of his hair or the size of his shoes.

For me it had never been that easy.

I was a small town boy who had escaped to the big city to pursue a more romantic life. Where I was from being gay was not so readily accepted, and once you'd slept with x, y and z, you were out of options.

And now, now I had all the options open to me, but was still too damn afraid to make a move.

I run faster, pushing myself harder, wishing that when I'd left my small town I could have managed to leave that small town boy behind too.

When I walk past his apartment, still breathing hard, I notice his door is open and there are boxes piled up outside. I have a flash of panic, breathing even harder, what if he's moving before I have the chance to act on my crush?

79

I stop, pretending to stretch my hamstrings, hoping that he'll catch sight of me and come to talk.

Because he does talk to me, a lot. My crush is based on more than the purely physical, it's also how he will tell me about his day at work when he sees me, tell me about what his so cute but mischievous cat has been up to, tell me what those delicious aromas are that are coming from his apartment. More than once he's asked me in for dinner, but though I want to say yes, every time I come up with some excuse, until now he's stopped asking me.

It's a very one-sided conversation, he talks to me, and at times I even think he's flirting, while I stammer and blush, flushed and flustered.

But if he's moving out maybe it's time for that to change.

'Hey, Matt!' he calls out, spotting me from where he's taping up boxes in his lounge.

'Morning, Josh, what you up to?'

'Having a clear out,' he tells me, and my pulse slows slightly, it's OK, he's not leaving. 'You want a drink?'

This is usually where I run away, but this time, I don't.

'Sure,' I tell him, not sure who's more surprised at my answer, him or me.

I sit on the sofa as he goes over to the fridge, throwing me a bottle of water before reaching back in for one of his own.

Now I'm not so panicked I look at him properly; he's wearing jeans, and they fit as well as I'd imagined.

Perhaps it's a sign.

'I'm glad to see you,' he continues, 'I was going to

come by later, ask for a favour. I have a box on top of my closet that I can't reach, thought you might be able to help me?'

'Sure,' I tell him, and though I'm still stuck on senseless one-word-answers, it's OK. I'm still sat in Josh's apartment, having a drink, and I'm going to help him.

It's good.

'It's through here,' he says, and I stand to follow him.

I can't believe I'm standing in Josh's bedroom.

It's clean and tidy, decorated in dark masculine colours, and the bed is huge, dominating the room. My eyes seem stuck to it, imagining us lying in it, tangled together, and I have to fight to tear my gaze away.

I drain my bottle, hoping that will help me cool down.

It doesn't help.

Instead it gets worse, as I look at his bedside table. There's lube and a box of tissues there, and immediately I picture him lying on his back, his jeans pulled down around his hips, his fist tight around his thick cock as he pumps at it intently.

My cock hardens immediately at the thought, and knowing my arousal is more than obvious in my flimsy running shorts, I try to think of disgusting things, my times tables, cleaning the bathroom, anything to make it disappear.

As the blood leaves my cock it seems to rush straight to my face, and though Josh may not have noticed my erection, he soon notices my blushing. He looks over at the lube, then away, choosing to spare me further embarrassment by ignoring that I've seen.

Instead he points to the top of his wardrobe.

'It's just up there. Shall I get you another bottle?'

I nod gratefully, glad of the opportunity to be alone for a second. I sit on his bed as he leaves, then get up just as quickly, if I sit here too long my imagination could go into such overdrive I won't be able to stand again.

So I reach for the box.

It's not a stretch for me, being a few inches taller than Josh, but even so it's far enough away that when I finally manage to pull it towards me, it breaks, spilling its contents across the floor.

'Shit!' I gasp, falling to my knees, trying to push everything back inside before Josh sees what I've done.

The box is broken so badly it isn't going to happen.

Then I actually look at the contents.

I'd thought initially, in my blind panic, that they were photos, but now I see they're prints.

Of naked men.

They aren't porn, or if they are they're like no sort I've ever seen before, no bodies glistening with body oil, no close ups of hard cocks, no vivid arcs of spunk shooting across the page.

Instead they are more artistic, men kissing passionately, men tangled together, men undoubtedly engaged in fucking, but seeming more sensual and erotic than the graphic images I've seen before.

More arousing than anything I've seen before.

I sit on the bed and flick through them, my cock almost throbbing now with the blood pumping through it, my running shorts tenting as every new image increases my excitement.

I realise Josh is taking an awful long time to fetch that water.

I look up, and he's stood in the doorway, watching me.

I want to apologise for the mess I've made, for looking at his photos, but there is no way I can speak right now.

Instead I am mute as his sits beside me and reaches for my cock, stroking me softly through the flimsy material.

Slowly he undresses me, taking his time as if at any minute I might flee, realising that this is not who I am.

But this *is* who I am.

I lie back on the bed, watching as he tenderly strokes each piece of skin that is exposed, until I am lying there naked.

His fingers trail across my shoulder, my collar bone, stroking the sensitive skin of my neck. Then they move lower, tangling in my chest hair, pausing at my nipples to tease and tweak.

I gasp, shifting on the bed, and he smiles, watching my cock bobbing for his attention.

He moves to kiss one nipple, then trails his tongue across my chest as he moves to kiss the other, leaving my chest hair matted like a mark of where he has been. I haven't felt his mouth on mine yet, but his lips on my chest leave me squirming with pleasure and anticipation.

Next he trails his hand down my stomach, then, reaching for the lube, quickly greases his hand and coats my shaft.

I'm helpless under his touch.

'You're such a little slut,' he says affectionately. 'Lying there and letting me do what I want to you.'

But now he is wrong; I'm no delicate flower to be treated so sensitively.

I want passion, not patience, lust, not longing.

I sit quickly, annoyed at my easy submission, of his gentle treatment of me.

I like it rough.

His smug smile is shaken when I grab him, and we are almost wrestling as we fall back on to the bed, fighting to be on top until I have him pinned beneath me.

Then I kiss him hard, until he is writhing against me, his clothed body rubbing against my bare skin, until he is breathless beneath me.

It feels as if a force of nature is unleashed.

His tongue is in my mouth, his legs entangled with mine, as I pull at his clothes, not caring if I rip them in my desire to get him naked.

I want to pause to find his tattoo, to admire his body, the smooth skin, the taut muscles, the hard cock, but let my hands do the exploring as they travel over his flesh, too excited to pause for even a second.

I reach for the lube, slicking my palm before I reach for his swollen cock, our bodies slick as we rub against each other, trying to find the best position to touch, to tease, to explore.

His hand is fast and furious, working me to a frenzy, even as his other hand travels lower, cupping my balls briefly, before his fingers slide lower, stroking the sensitive skin between balls and ass.

I want to suck him, fuck him, have him inside me, but I can't stop now, can't pull away now as his hand pumps at my cock, as his finger slips inside my hole, making me gasp loudly.

My hands follow his example, my finger teasing inside him, my fist gripping him hard, until I feel him spurting across my stomach.

It's all I need to take me over the edge, and I come hard, shaking violently.

Some time later I roll over, watching him doze with his hands above his head, admiring the muscles bulging in his arms. I find the tattoo.

Then I think things over.

There was no way he couldn't have managed those boxes on his own. Although I'm a few inches taller the boxes weren't dusty, and who puts their wank stash where they can't reach it easily?

Especially if you're the kind of guy who makes sure that lube and tissues are so convenient.

All it would have needed was some loose sellotape and good timing.

'This was a set up, wasn't it?'

'Mmm hmm,' he agrees sleepily. 'I thought you needed motivating.'

I smile, flattered. Now I have something even better to run back to.

Basic Rules of Anal Sex
by Kay Jaybee

I re-read the piece of paper that had been shoved into my hand, aware I was being watched carefully as my eyes travelled down the sheet. This was not new information, so why had he given it to me?

A Beginner's Basic Rules of Anal Sex
1.Start small.
2.Start slow.
3.Condoms and lube are your best friends.
4.Shit is part of life. Get used to it or forget it.
5.First time – one finger.
6.Second time – two fingers.
7.Stomach cramp is normal.
8.Third time – small anal dildo or butt-plug.
9.Fourth time – "For fuck's sake shaft me."

A Submissive's Basic Rules of Anal Sex
10. Do as you're told.
11. If no gag is provided, then bite the pillow.
12.If there is nothing to bite into, then scream.
13.It's only blood and crap. You'll live.
14.Expect to have to accommodate candles, dildos and fake horse tails, as well as his dick/her strap-on.
15.Remember to say "Thank you."

A Master's Basic Rules of Anal Sex
16. "Bend over bitch."
17. "Now!"

I looked from the typed white A4 sheet to the man who'd passed it to me, as I entered the nightclub. At first, I'd assumed he was giving out flyers to everyone, but he had no others in his hand, and as I glanced around, I saw no evidence of anyone else holding one.

Although I'd been to gay clubs in the past, this was my first visit to one since my recent move to London. It was so big and busily intimidating compared to those I'd been to before. The nerves, that I'd forced myself to ignore as I queued alone to enter the thunderously loud over-neon environment, hadn't waned as I'd hoped they would, and, as the paper creased in my grasp, my palms took on a clammy sheen.

'It's your first time in here, isn't it?'

I nodded dumbly at the stranger as I stood at the side of the bar.

'You want a drink?'

Nodding again, I wished I could think of something witty to say, but as he probably wouldn't have heard me over the hammer of the music's back-beat, I didn't bother, and simply watched him dive into the throng clamouring at the bar for a drink.

Folding the piece of paper up, I shoved it into my pocket, and examined the back view of my queuing assailant more closely. He was a little under average height, about five foot six perhaps, of fairly slim build, neatly cropped hair, blue jeans and a black T-shirt. In other words, he was interchangeable with nearly half the 20-something population that danced and chatted around me. In fact, from behind, but for the colour of his hair (ginger, rather than brown), he might have been me.

It wasn't until he turned around, that I realised how much I'd been distracted by the list he'd pressed into my hand. How come I hadn't noticed how attractive he was, how wide his green eyes were, and how mischievously his smile played at the corners of his mouth? As I took the pint of lager he offered me, I noticed his heavily freckled arms, and I found myself wondering how far those freckles spread over the rest of his body.

I clawed back my concentration; he was introducing himself by yelling the name, 'Jack' over the din. Then, after taking a swig from his pint, he pulled the paper back out of my pocket, fished a pen from his own, and scribbled an email address at the bottom of it, along with the words, *You're a submissive right? I bet you'd like it rough.* Then he disappeared into the crowd, leaving me alone with my drink.

Standing still for a second, I craned my neck, trying to find Jack again, but it was impossible to spot him amongst all the other T-shirted, short haired men. I wanted to ask him why he'd given me that list, why not just his name and email? Was he just being nice to me as I was obviously alone, or was he trying to scare me? Maybe he fancied me? I told myself I didn't really care about the reason (even though I did a bit, he *was* pretty cute), and was simply pleased I'd made my first social contact in the Capital, however bizarre.

I left the club shortly afterwards. Suddenly it seemed pointless to hang around on my own, and anyway I wanted to examine Jack's *Basic Rules* in private. I couldn't stop wondering how he'd worked out I was a submissive just like that. I mean, I *am* a submissive, and yes, I do like it a bit rough, but I didn't think I had that sort of information tattooed across my forehead.

It was so clinical, how he'd written it all down. Was Jack like that in bed? Did he fuck to a list? I felt my dick stirring at the thought of being under his control, and glanced at the laptop that sat on the muddled desk in the corner of my tatty rented bed-sit. Taking a deep breath, ignoring the voice at the back of my head telling me I was wasting my time as I'd never hear back from him, I typed a brief message.

Thanks for pint Jack. Meet sometime? Rob (guy you gave list to tonight).

The following morning two emails were waiting for me. The first had been sent about 2 a.m.

You know the gay bar in Richmond? Today, about 12 p.m?

The second had arrived just after 7 a.m.

I keep thinking about fucking you.

My stomach instantly knotted into a tense ball as I replied in the positive, before completely failing to relax for the rest of the morning. Jack's freckled arms monopolised my imagination, as I mentally began to trace them across his shoulders, his chest, his legs and his arse, like an erotic dot-to-dot. Would they reach his dick? As an image of Jack, naked and hard, grew in my mind, I ran to the bathroom. Roughly wanking myself off across the bath, I visualised this freckled man ordering me to do whatever he wanted, forcing my arse to accommodate no end of objects, just as the list had suggested.

I was relieved to see that the bar wasn't busy when I arrived at ten minutes to twelve, and I easily found a table for two. Ordering a coffee, I sat down, hoping like hell that Jack wouldn't be too long, for ever since my morning's masturbation, my thoughts had ranged uncontrollably from mildly kinky daydreams about him, to fantasies of extreme domination.

I was halfway through my scalding black liquid when he arrived. Spotting me straight away, Jack flicked a persuasive glance towards the door, 'You want to drink that, or you want to come back with me now?'

Clattering my cup into its saucer without a word, I followed Jack's retreating back in silence, my heart hammering in my chest. As we strode up the street my eyes kept wandering to his arse. It was neat and tight in his faded denims, and my throat dried at the prospect of what I desperately hoped was about to happen.

Jack wordlessly led me down a narrow side street, before fishing a key out of his pocket and shoving it unceremoniously into the front door of an old terrace house. I followed him into a poky damp hallway, lit by an insufficient light bulb.

That was when the potential stupidity of my actions hit me. I didn't know this man. I didn't really know where I was. I couldn't even be sure that Jack was really his name, or what he wanted from me. The perspiration of sexual anticipation that had been prickling my back, mingled with uncertainty as we stood outside another battered door. My brain was telling me to run, but my dick was telling me how cute Jack's arse was, and that I hadn't discovered the extent of his freckles yet.

As if reading my disquiet, Jack took my hand. His skin was soft, but his grip was firm as he pulled me through the doorway into his own tiny bed-sit. The pressure of Jack's touch, and the flash of passion that crossed his face as he stood in front of me, reassured me that I was right to be there after all. The lack of conversation however, was beginning to get on my nerves, 'Why the list?'

'First timers should get all the help they can.' Jack spoke with a flirty smile.

Suddenly I understood, 'Sorry to disappoint you, but it's not my first time. I mean, I'm not a virgin.'

Jack looked genuinely shocked, 'Really? Hell, you don't half look like one!'

I wasn't sure whether to be flattered or offended. 'That's hardly my fault is it? And anyway, if I was, that list of yours would have scared me to death!' As I spoke I wondered if my encounter with Jack was about to be cut abruptly short, 'I'm new to London, but not to all this.' Edging towards the door, I enquired hesitantly, 'You only go for virgins then?'

Jack laughed at my indignation, his expression twinkling with suggestion, 'No! But well, I guess I enjoy a bit of teaching every now and again.'

I felt some of the tension drain from my shoulders as I saw his playful grin, and I dared to move back a little closer to him, 'So you hover by the club door, and see if you can spot anyone who might benefit from some *Basic Rules* training?'

'Exactly.' The atmosphere between us took on a new intense edge as Jack took another step nearer to me, whispering, 'I guess we can dispense with the beginners' rules then. Do you want to practise some of the others instead? Some advanced training perhaps?'

My reply of, 'yes,' as he stretched a hand forward and ran a single finger across my cheek, was barely audible.

'Will you follow my rules? Will you do everything I tell you?'

Again I muttered, 'yes', my pulse rate shooting up as I regarded Jack's smoothly shaved face, his burning green eyes, and the enticing freckles that ran down his neck, disappearing tantalizingly beneath his white T-shirt.

He moved fast, as if he was afraid I'd change my mind. Something I couldn't have done if I'd wanted to, my cock was pressing so hard against my boxers that its needs had overtaken every vestige of my being.

'Strip.' Jack's voice cracked, his tone daring me to disobey. Fumbling with my clothes in my urgency, I was quickly naked, and felt myself being appraised by his piercing gaze. 'On your knees!'

I'd been anticipating the command, and dropped to the thinly carpeted floor.

'Close your eyes.'

I snapped them shut, shivering with cold and desire. As I waited, I clearly saw Jack's *Basic Rules* in my mind's eye, and hoped I'd be able to live up to his expectations.

'Open your mouth.'

I obliged, and was soon rewarded with the injection of a warm rigid dick. I gratefully ran my tongue over its length, licking the damp tip, relishing the salty, mildly sweaty taste, as Jack moved back and forth.

Jack pumped slowly at first, but then, with no warning, his pace increased to a ferocious pounding. He banged against my lips, burning my throat and straining my neck, as he treated my mouth as if it was my arse. I gagged and spluttered as he lunged; wishing he'd actually blindfolded me, as I fought to keep my eyes closed.

When he finally withdrew, I was left panting, dribbles of saliva and pre-come running down my chin. Remembering *Basic Rule no.15*, I swallowed to lubricate my voice and croaked, 'Thank you, sir,' and suddenly found myself thinking about his freckles again.

'Good boy.' Jack smoothed a hand through my hair with a tenderness of marked contrast to the previous few minutes. This temporary display of affection was short lived however, for 30 seconds later I was roughly slammed to the floor.

The second I was sprawled face down on the carpet,

Jack grasped my arms and tied them securely behind my back with some sort of binding. 'You will keep your eyes shut.'

'Yes, sir.'

'You will be punished for being so good.'

'Yes, sir.' No sooner had I agreed with him, than the first crack of leather, a belt I guess, smacked across my arse. I was unable to contain the shout that escaped my throat at the shock of this new attack.

'The more noise you make, the harder I will hit you.' Jack's voice was cold, but it had taken on an urgent edge, telling me exactly how turned on he was by my obedience.

I struggled to remain silent. The continuous burn of the strap was intense against my prone backside, and it took an incredible effort of will to obey him. Screwing my eyes up tighter, and digging my teeth into my lips so hard that they drew blood, I eventually managed to ride out two fierce strikes without uttering a sound.

A clatter told me that Jack had dropped his weapon to the floor, 'Well done, bitch, you're a fast learner.'

'Thank you, sir.' I licked away the droplets of blood that lingered on my lips, savouring the taste, as the bruised heat of my arse throbbed, and my swollen dick dug further into the carpet.

Abruptly, a hot moist tongue began to anoint my wounds. As Jack's delicious laps coated my injured flesh, my punished body dared to calm a little, but not for long, as a blunt jamming finger bit into my anus. This time however, I felt no shock, and gave no involuntary resistance. I wanted this. Oh fuck, did I want this!

Adhering to his own rules, Jack squeezed a drop of lube onto his fingers, and began to work it into me, first with one finger, then two, then three. Then I heard the rip of a condom packet, and my body tensed with the familiar sound of imminent satisfaction.

'Stand.' Jack whispered his words with a demanding hiss, as I clambered up clumsily, restricted by my bound wrists and lack of vision. I felt his cool hands manoeuvre me across the room, before he bellowed *Basic Rules no.16 and 17*, 'Bend over, bitch. Now!'

I bent, finding myself supported by the arm of a chair. My legs trembled as I braced myself for his invasion into my body, which I guessed would be rough and hard.

Nothing happened. Stillness came over the room, and as the seconds passed I began to panic. Maybe it hadn't been a condom packet I'd heard? Was Jack even still in the room? What was he doing? Should I open my eyes and see where he was? My mind raced and my dry throat felt raw as my stiff shoulders knotted further with the unexpected wait for action.

After what seemed an age, I heard another rip, as if something was being removed from tight packaging. 'I went shopping this morning.' Jack's tone was hoarse with want, 'I bought something I want to see up your arse.'

A frisson of fear crept over my spine.

'Would you like to see what it is?'

Despite my uncertainly I muttered, 'Yes, sir.'

'Very well, as you've been such a good boy you can open your eyes.'

As my vision adjusted to the dim light of the room, I focused on the object that the still-clothed, but obviously very turned-on Jack, waved in front of my face. I was instantly torn between relief that it wasn't a horsetail or a spiked dildo, and panic at the size of the incredibly thick rubber shaft that Jack cradled reverently in his hands, before obeying *Basic Rule no.3* and smearing its length with lube.

Obviously I've dreamt of the perfect dick, the massive cock that would fill every inch of me, but this was something else. Nine inches of solid black rubber. It must have been over two inches thick, and I could tell by the way that Jack was holding it, that it was heavy. My eyes literally began to water as I contemplated having Jack ram that thing into my anus. I'd been shagged by big blokes before, but this was going to hurt.

I opened my mouth to protest, but Jack interrupted my words before they even escaped my lips with a stinging palm slap to my butt.

'Remember the *Basic Rules,* Rob.' He produced a copy of the list, and held it up for me to see. 'Read *Rule no. 14* out loud.'

My voice quavered as I recited, '*Expect to have to accommodate candles, dildos and fake horse tails, as well as his dick/her strap-on.*'

Jack nodded with satisfaction. 'That's better. Now, shall we begin?'

I said nothing, my mind still refusing to see how my body would take such a thick rubber cock. My back passage tightened involuntarily at the mere thought.

As Jack lined the head of his new toy up against me, I struggled to calm my uneven breathing, closing my eyes again, unbidden this time, in an effort to concentrate.

Jack pushed, and the dildo crept into me a few centimetres. The sweat that had been dotting my forehead broke out properly, prickling my scalp and developing a sheen across my back. He shoved harder, and I gulped as my stomach cramped in accordance with *Basic Rule no. 7.* Then, blissfully, Jack slid a hand around my torso and grasped my cock, making me groan with semi-relief. Playing his fingers up and down my shaft, sometimes vigorously, sometimes with a teasing gentleness, he helped me to relax enough for him to drive the length a little further into my puckering channel.

I knew I couldn't take much more of this. Jack must have known it too, for he began to intensify his movements, forcing the dildo deeper and harder into me. My muscles cried out and my gut contracted and churned. I groaned and whimpered as I was opened wider and wider, my imagination filling with the picture my invaded backside must have created.

Basic Rules no. 4 and 13 from the list flew into my mind, and I suddenly feared that my bowels would spill as Jack kept urging the tool on. Would my skin split? This was brutal, and yet I knew that if he'd stopped now, I would have been more disappointed than relieved.

As Jack increased his pressure on my dick, with one sharp thrust, he plunged the remaining length of the dildo violently into me. With nothing to bite into, I adhered to Jack's *Basic Rule no. 12*, and screamed. I mean *really* screamed. My skin was pulling, and my muscles wrenched against the dragging weight of the rubber, as it was finally lodged securely in place.

Fuller than I had ever been, stretched to glorious, agonising capacity, with Jack still rubbing my cock, I couldn't hold on any longer, and released a long pent up yell. Asking through gritted teeth, just a little too late, for permission to come, I shot hot spunk across the armchair.

As Jack let go of me, my body shuddered and quivered, and I slumped against the furniture.

'Open your eyes.' Jack spoke quietly, and I opened them in time to see him strip before me. His beautiful dick, thick and hard, sprang up at me, and the freckles that had haunted me the night before assailed my blurred vision. They were everywhere.

Hastily, Jack untied my aching arms, all dominance

gone, as I rubbed some circulation back into my shoulders. 'You look fantastic with that up your arse. How does it feel?'

I murmured into his face, 'Incredible, mind-blowing, excruciating, wonderful.'

'You're amazing.' Jack kissed me, viciously, passionately, and I returned the gesture as he carefully eased the plug from my butt. Tears of pain gathered at the corners of my eyes, as the new toy dropped to the floor, and Jack dabbed my sore bruised arse with a cotton handkerchief.

When my ragged breathing began to steady, I pointedly regarded Jack's straining dick, and with a half smile said, 'I think it's your turn now. I don't suppose you have a felt-tip pen around here somewhere?'

Jack frowned, puzzled at my request, but his eyes shone with desire, 'Yes I have, why?'

'I know it isn't on your *Basic Rules* list or anything, but do you fancy a game of dot-to-dot?'

Safe and Sound
by Alex K. Bell

Muted sounds echoed around my head, only sometimes making sense, as I faded in and out of consciousness: strange scraping noises, sporadic crackles on a radio, soft drawn-out footsteps, and then an intense rushing sound, which unnerved me for a while, until I worked out it was the wind, which based on the flapping of the blankets wrapped tightly around me, was blowing up a storm.

I struggled desperately to recall where I was, and what I'd been doing, but came up with nothing. An intense throbbing grew inside my head, pounding my senses mercilessly, until I could take no more, and I fell into blackness.

By the time I came around again, my mind was racing, desperately trying to sort an overload of information, which was flooding back at an incredible rate. Fragmented images flashed across my mind, and facts, and maps and warnings competing at once for my attention. My head jerked side to side, as I desperately tried to make sense of it, and my body shook uncontrollably, until finally, mercifully, the blackness took me again.

I stirred suddenly, and feeling water beneath me, kicked out wildly, no comprehension of my surroundings, desperately trying to find purchase, to push myself to safety. Then success, as my foot found a thin hard edge. I locked my leg quickly, and forced myself upwards.

'Shhhhh, shhh, shhh, shhh there, son, it's OK ... you're OK,' came a deep soothing voice, close to my ear, which only served to confuse me more.

I kicked and writhed and twisted as best I could, but strong arms held me tight, and kept me still, until exhausted, my arms and legs stopped fighting, and I gave in, finally opening my eyes.

As the deep tones attempted to comfort and reassure me once more, my eyes flitted around a tiny shack, quickly taking in the fiercely roaring fire, the crude timber beds, and the mountain of electrical equipment in the far corner. Finally, my gaze dropped down, to look directly beneath me, where an old-fashioned iron bath sat, teeming with hot water, steam forming where the heat met the cool air of the room. Beside it was a freshly-boiled kettle, ready to top it up.

Partly because I'd convinced myself I was safe, but mostly because every bit of energy had disappeared from my body, I relaxed, and my body went limp. The big stranger holding me felt this, and he finished lowering me downwards, placing my torso ever so slowly and gently into the bath, the water immediately soothing and comforting my aching body. I let out a sigh of relief and of satisfaction, as the warmth enveloped me, only then realising how cold I was, and how much I was shaking. I had another panic attack, as more memories flooded back, causing my body to jerk and splash uncontrollably.

'Hey, hey, hey,' he said calmly, draping a towel around my shoulders. 'You're OK, son,' he assured, stroking a friendly hand on my head. 'You're safe and sound now.' His soft rich American voice calmed me immediately this time. Once I'd settled again, he slipped some thick towels between the back of my knees and the hard metal edge of the bath, making them more comfortable.

'Can't warm these yet,' he said quietly, doing the same with my arms, tucking towels under my armpits, then letting them ease back down. 'Not until your core's had a chance to warm up. Pushing cold blood from your arms and legs back into your torso can do some pretty bad things – *after-drop* the hypothermia books call it.'

I had to take his word for it. I was almost too exhausted to think. My torso slumping softly against the raised metal back of the bath, my head falling back to rest on a rolled-up towel considerately draped there. The sound of the fire crackling in the background, and the water sploshing softly against my chest was starting to soothe me. Then, in the click of a magician's fingers, my body went completely limp, and my eye-lids grew very heavy. I was aware of him talking somewhere in the background, but the words didn't stick, becoming less and less tangible with each heavy blink, until I fell into a deep, deep sleep.

My eye-lids twitched and I started to wake. I don't know how long I'd been out, maybe a few minutes, maybe an hour. But however long it was, it had definitely done me good. I knew that because I could now feel the pain deep in my limbs, as I flexed and stretched them. What was more positive was that the shaking from earlier had almost completely gone.

My gaze drifted to the fireplace, where my rescuer was throwing fresh logs onto the fire. The thick cold timber subdued the flames at first, but soon started to yield, as flames licked up around them, especially after he stoked the heart of the fire with a poker. As the flames grew, I used the flickering light to pick out his shape.

He was big, much bigger than me, and much bigger than the guys I usually go for. In many ways, he looked like an archetypal woodsman from a fairytale: tall; jet black hair; rugged face with accompanying chiselled chin; broad chest and shoulders; and arms – what arms.

An image popped into my head, of him striking a tree with an axe, felling it with just a handful of thunderous strikes. A fantasy figure definitely! It was while I considered this, my eyes darting all over his body, that I realised I was sporting a significant hard-on, thankfully for now hidden beneath the surface of the water.

Suddenly he turned, and caught me watching him. I was a bit embarrassed for a moment, until he smiled simply, and then walked over to me, clutching a freshly boiled kettle full of water.

'Should be fine now,' he said, placing the kettle to one side for a moment, then carefully lifting one of my legs, and placing it into the warm welcoming water. As I let out a long contented sigh, he did the same with the other leg, and then my arms. Because there wasn't enough room to straighten my legs, I kept them bent, my knees poking up through the water's surface.

'Watch your legs!' he urged, lifting the kettle over the foot of the bath. I complied, pulling my feet right back, until my heels pushed against my bum, only then registering that he'd placed me in the bath completely naked, and that at some point previous to that, had stripped me naked.

He carefully emptied the contents of the kettle into the water, sending out wonderful flows of heat that wrapped deliciously around my bare flesh, further soothing it.

'So what crazy urge lands an English kid like you 10,000 feet up, on one of the worst February days in

Sawatch Range history, son?' he asked, picking up a thick cloth from the side, and dipping it into the water.

I started to explain about my University course, studying Applied and Environmental Geology, and my industry-funded gap-year project documenting evolving extreme climates, but became distracted almost immediately when he began to run the hot, water-soaked cloth along one of my arms, water dripping noisily from it as he twisted and squeezed the cloth around my tender skin.

He nodded politely as I continued talking, squeezing the cloth tightly in his huge hand, straining the water from it, then plunging it deep beneath the water's surface, to soak up some more. This time, he drew the warm sopping cloth across my shoulder, firmly pressing along the tight muscles, sending, almost in slow-motion, rivulets of water dribbling down my chest and back. He stroked it back and forth along the top of my shoulder, then slid it up the side of my neck. Without realising, I tilted my head to the side, to give the cloth, and his hand, more access. The warmth of the water, and the rhythmic movements of his hand, made my mouth fall open, and I let out a deep satisfied moan.

'Good?' he asked, moving the cloth ever so slowly around the back of my neck to the other shoulder. I only managed to nod, mouth gaping still. Then he reached forward, dunking the cloth down in front of my chest, directly over my crotch, only narrowly missing my increasingly-stiffening cock, before pulling it back out, and stroking it in a seemingly sensuous motion, round and around my chest. My heart beat fast in my chest as he worked, so softly, so tenderly, despite his obvious strength and size.

'Lucky for you your phone held out so long,' he said

softly, continuing the hypnotic circles on my chest, the edge of the cloth occasionally catching a nipple, making them stiffen. 'Batteries held just long enough for me to hone in on you,' he added, matter-of-factly. 'Took close on two hours.'

My breathing grew heavy as his fingers worked, just the thin crushed cloth separating them from my wet naked flesh. After straining and rinsing the cloth a few times, he lifted it up and slipped it slowly across my face, perfectly moulding the warm cloth around my features. 'Then another three hours ... maybe four, to get you back here.' He dunked his hand down again, brushing against my twitching belly, achingly close this time to my cock. 'No helicopters flying tonight, son. Not with the wind like it was.'

But I couldn't think about helicopters, or rescue, or gratitude ... all I wanted was for him to drop the cloth, reach down into the water, and wrap his strong fingers around my cock, which was now throbbing incessantly.

Instead, he dropped the cloth at my side, then eased my torso forward. After picking up the cloth again, water flowing freely from it, he slopped it onto my exposed back, then started to rub it firmly around. Using firm broad strokes, he smoothed his hand across each shoulder-blade, masterfully pushing away any tension, before tracing down the length of my spine, forcing the cloth quite a way beneath the water, where it brushed teasingly at the top of my bum. His body was close to mine, his manly scent, of hard earned sweat, and machinery oil, and the thick tangy odour of freshly cut mountain pines, was completely intoxicating. When finished, he returned my torso, to rest once more against the warm metal back of the bath.

My chest heaved almost uncontrollably now, as I

fantasised about the two of us in an embrace: hands searching, lips kissing, buttons popping, hot flesh in hand, teasing, stroking, rubbing, wanking … then gasping lips parting, split by male flesh, mouth warm and inviting, cock pushing deeper and deeper inside.

At some point, I couldn't remember when, I'd started to slide my hand along my cock, relishing the feel of it, enjoying my fingers wrapped tightly around it, tell-tale ripples and splashes on the water's surface telegraphing what I was doing.

He seemed not to notice, and stood up calmly. 'You're good to soak for a few minutes,' he said, heading back to the fire, where he threw on a few more logs, enough to last us the night. 'There are some towels on the seat beside you,' he said quietly, 'whenever you're done.'

I closed my eyes, slowing my hand a little, as the new logs started to crack and spit as the flames rapidly took hold. I should be thinking about the bigger picture now, how lucky I was to be alive, how grateful I was for my rescue, how great it will be when I get to see my friends and family, but all I could think about was the stranger's big hands just a few moments ago, stroking my chest with slow sensuous movements, water flowing and dribbling slowly from the cloth, the hard sewn edge just catching my nipples, making them visibly swell. I sighed to myself, imagining he was still doing it, and then pictured his hand plunging much deeper into the water, where he twisted the cloth between my belly and my cock, knowingly teasing me.

I imagined grabbing his wrist as it cleared the water, shaking it firmly until his grip was broken and he dropped the cloth, then I plunged his hand deep into the water, where his fingers automatically locked on to my throbbing manly flesh, stroking along its length, his hand slow, strong, experienced. I thrust my cock upwards, fucking it into his imaginary hand.

My eyes snapped open, and scanned the room. He was at one of the small beds, loading it with heavy sheets and quilts. I took in his body again, only this time more lustfully, and while stroking my cock. His muscles rippled and tensed beneath his tight shirt as he shook out the sheets, then tossed them across the bed. Then he gave me a perfect view of his tight bum as he stooped to tuck in the corners. I had no idea who he was, whether he was a hunter, or a ranger, or just someone who wanted to get away from it all, up here in the beautiful but hazardous mountains. But what I did know was that he was turning me on more than any man ever had. I wanted to make a move ... I had to make a move.

Gripping the edge of the old metal bathtub tightly, I locked my arms and started to push myself up, only moments later realising just how exhausted I was. My arms shook, but stayed locked, as I struggled to stand upright. My head, which had started to feel very light, flopped helplessly down, serving only to present me with a view of my stiff twitching cock, shining strangely in the firelight, as water from my torso flowed down along its length and streamed from the tip, splashing noisily into the bathwater. But I didn't give up, and managed to lock my knees, then straighten my back a little – before the blood completely drained from my head, and I started to faint. I slumped heavily backwards, my bum just catching the back of the bath, as my locked legs struggled to support me, and my arms flailed wildly, knocking the empty kettle to the floor. A split-second later his arms were around me once again, holding me up, holding me close.

'You're gonna have to take it a little slower there, son,'

he laughed, sweeping me up in his arms, and carrying me to the bed he'd just been making. 'There'll be plenty of time for *Mr Independent* later on.'

My head was reeling, partly from nearly fainting moments earlier, but mostly from being held so tightly by him, my naked body crushed firmly against his. He laid my glistening form gently down on my side, with my back to the edge of the bed, and draped a thick towel across my torso.

'Here you go; get yourself dried,' he urged, 'before you get cold. I need to empty that tub.' And he turned to walk away.

'Wait!' I said quickly, my mind racing. He stopped in his tracks. For a long moment, he just stood there, his back to me.

'Would you ... could you ... dry me?' My voice descended to a whisper.

Still he stood there.

'You're right, I must rest,' I added.

I heard his weight shift on his heels. What would he say?

'It's the last thing I'll ask of you tonight,' I said, heart racing madly. 'I promise.'

Again, he shifted on his heels, then made my heart sink, as he started to walk away, but then skip a beat, as he stopped once more, clearly weighing up the possibilities.

Then next thing I knew he'd lifted the towel from my body, then after a tense moment, he started to rub my back. His hands pushed the towel smoothly and firmly, moving it in simple broad arcs, spiralling circles and soothing strokes, blending seamlessly between them, as he dried my upper back and shoulders. My body rocked naturally beneath him, as he pressed the coarse towelling firmly against my body. A shiver ran down my spine as the towel stroked my neck, firmly pressing along the back and the sides, then smoothly down my lower back and hip, and across the muscled globes of my bum, where the towel lingered, cupping and squeezing my rounded flesh until they were completely dry. I couldn't stop myself from twisting and writhing against his hand, just the towelling separating his stroking, soothing fingers from my naked, quivering flesh.

He slid the towel along the back of my thighs, long undulating strokes caressing my skin, before pressed the towelling between them, easing my thighs a touch apart, allowing his hand to slide higher and higher, closer to my crotch. My thighs parted almost without thinking, allowing him more access. His hand reached the top, the towel drying the very tops of my inner thighs, the loose material glancing gently against my balls as he worked. Then he moved quickly downwards again, drying the backs of my knees, and sliding the towelling across my calves and ankles, brisk firm strokes until he reached my feet. He wrapped the towel around each in turn, and rubbed them firmly with both hands, making them warm as well as dry. Then he pushed the towelling between my toes, drying each of the gaps between them.

After placing my feet gently down, he moved back up the bed, to stand beside my torso. Neither of us spoke, but I knew it was time for me to turn onto my back. My heart raced ten-to-the-dozen as I readied myself. I shifted my weight, then slowly turned over. I felt a rush of excitement, and a touch of vulnerability, as my back finally settled on the mattress, and my head came to rest comfortably on the pillow. My naked body now lay completely exposed to his gaze. My eyes drifted down my body, to take in what his eyes undoubtedly were, my heaving chest, my trembling stomach, which disturbed the water pooled in my belly-button, and just a bit down from there, my cock, was sticking right up to attention, twitching almost uncontrollably as wicked thoughts flashed across my mind. A tiny drop of transparent fluid leaked from the tiny slit at the tip. I turned my head to look up into his face, his rugged handsome features more visible in this light. I caught him staring into space, looking *anywhere* but my cock. But his arousal was indisputable, as evidenced by his quickened breaths, and dry lips, which he fixed with a flash of his broad tongue.

He seemed dumbstruck for a moment, his eyes flickering wildly from the firelight, his mind racing surely. Then suddenly he snapped into action, reaching for a fresh towel at the foot of the bed, then after leaning in close, he started to dry my chest and shoulders.

Despite the air being filled with erotic tension, his hands moved just as firmly, just as steadily, in broad deliberate circles, sweeping the soft towelling across my skin, leaving a trail of goosebumps in its wake. He lingered at each nipple, circling around and around them, moving closer with each caress, until his fingers brushed against them, making them stand up for us both to see, and making my cock twitch in appreciation. Then he eased the towel down across my belly, which spasmed erratically in response, my cock just inches now from his swirling hand ... but he didn't falter, didn't get distracted.

He stiffened one of his fingers, then pressed gently through the towel, and started spiralling in towards my belly button, deliberately slowly, excruciatingly so, until he slipped it inside and he soaked up the water there. His fingertip pushed deep, making me writhe and buck helplessly beneath him. With it still inserted, he pressed delicately around the outside of the little hole, arousing me further, as the loose part of the towel brushed roughly against the shaft of my cock, firing off an jolt of erotic energy, making my balls tighten, and setting off a throbbing pulsing heat deep in my gut. The sensation, and the anticipation of him moving his skilled hands further down my body, was driving me mad, and making me moan out loud, and causing me to jerk my crotch upwards.

Then his finger slipped out, and he started zig-zagging the towel down my lower belly. I gasped, flicking my head to the side, when I noticed his jean-clad crotch closer than expected, a huge bulge trapped behind his trouser buttons. I couldn't resist. I reached up with both hands, and started popping the buttons, one by one, as he slipped the towel along the soft flesh where my leg met my crotch, sliding down deep, then slowly back up, where he teased at the edge of my pubic area.

I popped the last button on his jeans, and quickly tugged down his underwear, to reveal a thick, delectable looking cock. I wasted no time, and gripping the opening in the jeans with both hands, I pulled his crotch towards me, and his cock slipped straight inside my mouth. I felt him tense and his hand falter for a moment, as I started sucking lovingly on the head of his cock, a thick bulbous plum with a soft velvety texture. I moaned as I flattened my tongue and licked all around it like a lollypop, tasting it, relishing it.

He dabbed at my pubic hair, soaking up the glistening beads of water entangled there, the edge of the towel still brushing my cock, making it throb and twitch even more, come starting to boil up deep inside me. Then the towel slipped lower, reaching the base of my cock, then cruelly, he sidestepped it, sliding straight down and along the top of my thigh, in a slow firm deliberate movement.

I pulled my mouth back and kissed and sucked the tip, lathering it with my saliva, making unashamedly disgusting noises with my lips and mouth. Then I flicked a stiffened tongue tip across the tiny slit, exquisite feather-light touches, which made him grunt and fuck his cock back inside my warm mouth. I accepted it willingly, and slid my lips up and down the shaft, perfectly meeting his thrusts.

The towel slipped down my calf, across my feet, then to the other calf, up which it proceeded to slide slowly upwards.

I wrapped my fingers around the thick flesh of his cock, and wanked it into my welcoming mouth, my fist in perfect synch with my plunging lips. My tongue licked side to side along the base when it was buried deep inside my mouth, then I slurped wantonly on the soft delicate tip when at my lips again, making him grunt and curse almost constantly.

The towel moved up past my knee and up my other thigh, until it reached my crotch where for a moment, it teased around the base of my cock. Then finally, his fingers gripped my stiff flesh through the towel, twisting his hand around it.

I gasped around his cock, then quickened my mouth. It wouldn't be long before I came, and I wanted us to come together. He jerked his hips harder in return, as overcome with arousal as I was, making me moan in appreciation around his cock.

Finally he threw the towel aside and wrapped his strong fingers around my cock. I gasped as flesh finally touched flesh, and my hips jerked off the bed to meet the long strokes of his fist, his tight grip catching my swollen head as I pulled it back again, causing an incessant throbbing heat to start surging up from my balls.

I blurred my fist on his shaft, and sucked ravenously at his head, as his hips bucked helplessly, as he started losing control. Any second now ... any second now! Then my mouth gaped wide in shock, allowing his cock to nudge at the back of my throat, after he'd jammed his lips down around my pulsing cock, taking it deep inside his hot, wet mouth.

I squeezed my lips tight around his cock and started jamming my mouth fast and hard along its length, my lips sucking and slurping noisily, saliva pooling and stringing from my lips as I consumed his hot flesh.

He matched me perfectly, quickly bobbing his head up and down on my cock, taking my twitching flesh deep in his mouth then back out again, lips gripping tightly, slicking it with his spit.

Our hands worked in unison, furiously wanking each other's cock into our mouths, moaning our own pleasure around the pulsating cockheads. I could feel my come rising, shooting up from my balls. My actions stuttered, then the tip of my cock exploded. He locked his lips tight around my shaft as I ejaculated hard and fast into his waiting mouth. He moaned his appreciation as jet after jet hit the back of his throat. I moaned as I came, still able to lick hungrily at the cockhead buried in my mouth. This was too much for him too, and he jerked his hips one last time, then his cock stiffened, and unloaded into my mouth, copious amounts, further encouraged by my lips, sucking wantonly on his twitching flesh, milking from him as much as I could.

Another shot of spunk hit his licking tongue as he continued to fill my mouth. We were locked in a moment of pure ecstasy, cocks jerking and spurting together, mouths wanting and welcoming. Then suddenly ... we had nothing left, and collapsed together on the bed, the quilts falling over us, where we lay huddled for some time, until we both drifted off to sleep.

Kit Bag
by J L Merrow

Black Muscle Vest and Grey Sweats were in again, which was kind of odd. Kit hadn't seen them in the gym on a Saturday night before. Saturday mornings were their thing, and Monday and Wednesday evenings, regular as clockwork. Always together, although he still couldn't figure out if they were *together* together.

He watched them walking over to the weights, slow and easy. They looked just perfect together; one fair, one dark, like those pop groups put together by a designer. Black Muscle Vest was the dark one, of course. Black was just the *only* colour for him to wear. He had close-cropped raven hair and soft brown skin Kit was just aching to touch. He knew exactly which bit too. And it wasn't the obvious one, oh, no. That man had just the most *amazing* trapezius muscles. Kit got all shivery just looking at those incredible bulges between neck and shoulder. He wanted to run his hands all over them, learn their contours by touch. Worship them.

Sometimes he almost thought Black Muscle Vest might go for that too, if he could only get him on his own. But Grey Sweats was always there too, beautiful but unapproachable, like a Norse God with his pale skin, blond hair and strong jaw. He had that whole don't-mess-with-me vibe that sent shivers down Kit's spine.

Kit watched them spot each other on the weights for a while, wishing he could get a closer look. Then he had a light-bulb moment – the elliptical up that end was looking like it *really* needed a wipe-down. Kit took a bucket and cloth and headed on up there.

Black Muscle Vest was lying on the bench, pressing some totally unfeasible weight. He was so pumped up from the workout Kit would have sworn those biceps were larger around than Kit's waist. There was a spreading damp patch across his vest, and perspiration stood out in beads on the visible portion of his chest. Kit would've given a kidney to be able to lick that off. A testicle, even. He swallowed, and tried to remember at least to pretend to be cleaning the elliptical.

Black Muscle Vest dropped the bar back on the supports with a muted clang, and sprang off the bench. 'Let's see you beat that, you lightweight,' he teased Grey Sweats.

'Any time, wuss,' Grey Sweats threw back at him, and he lay down on the bench over the damp outline Black Muscle Vest had left on the vinyl covering. Kit squirmed a little, thinking how much he'd have liked to do that. Lie down, and get himself all messy in Black Muscle Vest's sweat. Oh, Lord. Now he was going to have to go back and hide behind the desk so they couldn't see he'd got hard.

Damn. And pretty soon they'd be finishing up and heading for the showers. Kit gave a little sigh. What he wouldn't have given to go down there with them. He could have offered to scrub their backs, or give them a really thorough clean with his tongue ... Sometimes, Kit wished he'd been born earlier. Say, 2,000 years, give or take. He could have been a Roman bath house slave. He'd have been a *good* slave. He'd have had a cute little tunic,

114

with maybe some pretty braid – nothing too fancy, though, because, hello, *slave* – and it'd be just a little bit too short. Because the Romans may have invented scissors, socks and satire, but they'd never quite got around to boxer shorts, so every time Kit bent over everyone would get a peek at his sexy little butt.

He'd have waited for those hunky gladiators to come in from the training grounds, all sweaty and dirty, and he'd have poured oil over their hot bodies and massaged it in, soothing away the aches from those big, strong muscles. Then he'd have got his strigil (and Kit did actually have a strigil, he'd found one in a sex shop and it was his prized possession, although he wasn't quite sure right now where he'd put it) and scraped their skin clean, before leading them to the baths for a nice hot rinse.

After that he'd have asked breathily, 'Is there anything else you require, sir?' And they'd have bent him over the massage bench and fucked him until he couldn't see straight.

Kit sighed, and thanked the Lord he was safe behind the desk. His gym-issue sweatpants were pretty smart for what they were, and they were tight enough to show off his ass nicely, but oh, man, they didn't hide a thing. They certainly didn't hide *Kit's* thing, sticking out proudly in front of him and pointing straight at Black Muscle Vest and Grey Sweats.

At least it was late enough there was no one else around. Just Kit and his two fantasies-made-flesh, and damn, thinking of their flesh was not going to help him regain control. Kit looked down at his desk, trying to remember how to read the papers spread across it. It was time to close up, actually, but Kit figured he could wait until Black Muscle Vest and Grey Sweats had finished. He'd have to wait, because going over there to tell them it was time to pack up would involve, well, going over there to tell them it was time to pack up, and embarrassment aside, he still wasn't certain they were gay. Not that he'd ever tried anything so dumb, but Kit figured approaching a couple of big, beefy straight guys with a hard-on for them would be one hell of a bad idea.

'Good night, then,' a low voice called, startling Kit and making him drop the pencil he'd been fiddling with.

'Oh!' he cried, looking straight up into Black Muscle Vest's deep brown eyes. 'Yes! I mean, good night. Thank you.' Kit wanted to curl up in embarrassment. They must think he was such a jerk.

Black Muscle Vest just smiled, and sauntered out through the turnstile, his arms held out from his body by the sheer volume of muscle, and man, wasn't that a sight? Grey Sweats was already gone, and Kit *really* needed to stop getting so distracted. He tidied up his desk, locked up the gym and headed down the stairs.

Black Muscle Vest was still in his sweaty gym kit, just leaning against the wall next to the changing room door. His arms were trying to fold but were too damn big to manage it. 'Got a problem in the changing rooms,' he said. 'I think you'd better take a look.'

'Is it the showers again? Darn it, we only had the plumber in last week! I am going to be so mad if those drains are clogged again already.' Did it sound like he was babbling? Black Muscle Vest's face was like granite, if you could get granite in the exact shade of tan of a leather jacket Kit had used to own, which he doubted. Had they noticed Kit looking at them? Was he about to get into the worst trouble of his life? 'Uh, maybe I should call someone? At reception, there'll be someone there still …'

Black Muscle Vest smiled. It was a friendly smile, Kit

116

thought. Not a we're-going-to-give-you-such-a-kicking smile. He hoped. 'Oh, I think you can handle it,' Black Muscle Vest said slowly. 'Unless you're telling me you're not man enough for the job?'

Kit felt a little shiver pass through him. 'I'll, uh, I'll take a look, shall I?'

He walked into the changing rooms, Black Muscle Vest so close behind him Kit could feel the moist heat coming off that sweaty body in waves. They went past the banks of lockers, and when they rounded the corner there was Grey Sweats.

Only he wasn't wearing his grey sweats any longer. He wasn't wearing *anything*, unless you counted a slow smile and the biggest hard-on Kit had seen in an age. Kit watched, caught like a bug on a slide, as Grey Sweats stroked himself lazily and asked, 'Think you can do anything about this?'

'Oh,' Kit breathed. 'Oh, Lord ...' He couldn't seem to get any more words out, but he figured his dick was doing the talking for him. There it was, pointing straight out in front of him like a little kid going 'Look-at-it, Mommy!'

'I'm Sven. In case you were interested,' Grey Sweats said teasingly.

'You, uh, you look like a Sven,' Kit managed. 'The blond ... hair.' And Lord, didn't he just? Like a Viking about to rape and pillage. Kit was going all goose-bumpy at the thought.

'And I'm Harry,' Black Muscle Vest rumbled in Kit's ear, as a meaty hand fondled his ass.

'Kit,' Kit told them. 'It's short for Christopher, but everyone calls me Kit. Guess it's because I'm small. Need a short name.'

'You don't look small from where I'm standing,' Sven murmured, appreciation in his voice.

117

Kit swallowed, as his dick did its damnedest to prove Sven right.

'I think we need to see just how big he is, Harry,' Sven said, coming towards them. 'I think we need to take all his clothes off, and have a really good look.'

Kit felt his sweatpants being pushed over his hips along with his underwear, until his cock caught slightly on the elastic and then bobbed up as it was freed. He whimpered. Harry pushed the clothes all the way down to Kit's ankles and left them there, then pulled his T-shirt up and over his head. For a moment Kit wondered if Harry was going to leave that there too, leave him blinded as well as hog-tied, and he shuddered, but Harry pulled it right off and slung it on the low bench. Kit saw there was already a thick towel laid out on the bench, and he felt a deep thrill tingle up from his toes.

'We've seen you watching us, Kit,' Harry told him, beefy hands now moving up to pinch Kit's nipples, making his eyes water and his cock throb. 'And we know what you've been thinking. Admit it, Kit. You're a dirty, dirty little boy, aren't you?'

'I bet you've been dreaming of something like this, haven't you?' Sven stepped up close until Kit felt like a thin slice of white bread between two hunks of beef, kind of like a sandwich in reverse. He whimpered at the sensations of those two cocks jabbing into him while Harry carried on twisting his nipples so hard Kit's toes curled.

'I bet you'd love it if we just bent you over that bench and took turns fucking you raw, wouldn't you?' Harry mused. 'I bet you'd be screaming for more. Little sluts like you always want more.'

'Oh, God! Yes, yes please ...' Kit felt his face grow red. He'd *never* behaved like this before. But Lord, he wanted to be their slut. Wanted them to take him and use him. And then use him some more. 'Please ...' He tried to twist in Harry's grasp – Sven's cock was just inches from his own erection, jabbing into his hip, and he wanted to feel its heat against his own so, so much ...

Sven stepped back, and Kit groaned in disappointment. 'Not so fast, Kit. You've got a decision to make.'

'I have?'

'Yeah,' Harry's voice buzzed in his ear. 'See, one of us is going to have that tight little ass of yours, and the other one's going to take your mouth.' As he spoke, he pushed down his black sweatpants. Kit moaned as a huge, thick cock sprang out, a mass of black wiry curls at its base. 'So what's it going to be, Kit? White meat or dark?'

Kit shivered. 'Dark,' he whispered.

Harry smiled. 'Good choice, Kit. Now get up on that bench.'

Kit kicked off his trainers and the clothes pooled around his ankles and scrambled to obey, kneeling down on the towel they'd left for him. His cock was so hard it hurt. He didn't dare touch it, though. What would they do to him if he touched himself? Mouth dry, Kit wondered if it might be worth finding out. Bracing himself on one arm, he reached slyly between his legs. Surely, Sven would have something to say about *that*.

Please let Sven have something to say about that.

Kit wasn't disappointed. He yelped as a big, hard hand slapped him painfully on the butt. 'None of that,' Sven growled. 'That's our property now. Dirty little boys who touch our property without permission are asking to be punished.' He rubbed his calloused hand roughly over Kit's still-stinging butt cheek.

'I think he needs something to distract him,' Harry commented. He moved forward to hold Kit's face between his hands. That enormous cock was just inches from Kit's nose, the musky, sweaty smell of it driving him wild, and his mouth dropped open automatically. 'Hungry, are you?' Harry laughed.

'Please,' Kit begged. He could have howled as Harry backed off a pace. But then he felt Sven kneading his butt cheeks, spreading them – and oh, Lord, that was his tongue, diving into Kit's ass and teasing his hole. Big hands gripped his hips, keeping them from moving as Sven's tongue flickered around Kit's entrance. Kit was horrified by the sounds he was making – wanton, needy sounds – as his whole body juddered, driven out of control by that slick, wet muscle. And when it speared inside him … if it hadn't been for those hands anchoring him like a vice, Kit would've leapt clean off the bench.

'Like that, do you, Kit?' Harry's voice seemed to come from far, far away. 'Do you like how he's opening you up? Better hope he does a good job, Kit. Going to be his cock in a minute and it's going to split you in half.'

'Please,' Kit gasped again. He opened his eyes and looked up at Harry. From this angle, he was all cock, and damn, Kit wanted to feel that inside him. He mewled as Harry stepped forward and rubbed his erection against Kit's cheek.

'I think he's ready for it,' Kit heard Harry say, and suddenly that wonderful, dark cock was jabbing against his lips, forcing them to open. Behind him – oh, Lord! Gagged by Harry's thick, hot cock, Kit could barely moan as Sven's erection pierced his ass and just kept on going.

'Fuck, that's good.' Sven sounded strained, and not quite in control any more. Had Kit done that? A rush of pride flooded him from his gut right up to his throat.

'Oh, yeah,' Harry panted as he thrust in and out of Kit's willing lips. Kit felt transported, like he didn't belong to himself any more. These two men owned him, body and soul. He was their slave, and maybe it'd kill him but damn, he'd die happy.

'Gonna come,' Harry grunted, and almost as soon as the words penetrated his pleasure-fogged brain, Kit tasted Harry's come in his mouth, salty, warm and thick, pulse after pulse of it surging into him. He drank it down greedily, determined not to spill a drop.

When Harry's softening cock slipped out of Kit's mouth, he felt the loss like it'd been part of him. But Sven was still thrusting in and out of his ass, nailing his gland and making him see stars. Kit was barely aware of Harry manoeuvring himself on the bench until suddenly he felt the incredible sensation of cool lips around his heated, needy erection, and he yelped with the shock and the pleasure of it. It was all too much, and Kit howled as he climaxed, every thrust of Sven's cock inside him driving him deeper into Harry's throat. The big man kept on sucking until Kit was utterly drained, swallowing him down just as Kit had done for Harry.

Then Kit felt Sven pull out, leaving him empty and hollow inside, and a moment later hot come spattered over his back and butt. Marking him. Claiming him. Kit was theirs, totally and completely. For as long as they wanted him. And he hoped it'd be for more than one night but even if this was all he was going to have, Kit figured he had nothing to complain about.

He felt a rough towel wiping him down, and strong hands helped him off the bench.

Harry was smiling at him. 'Dirty, dirty boy,' he murmured. It sounded like an endearment. Kit felt himself flush. Lord, even after all they'd done he still couldn't look the man in the eye.

'Do you need anything from your place?' Sven asked

as he threw Kit his shirt.

'My place?'

'We're taking you home with us,' Sven told him in a tone that brooked no argument. 'Dirty little boys like you aren't safe on their own.'

Kit yelped as Harry gave his ass a squeeze. 'This is ours now, and that wicked, dirty mouth of yours. Wouldn't want anything bad to happen to them. So, do we need to stop off at your place on the way?'

Kit struggled to make his brain work. He felt sated, and drained, and wonderful. He couldn't think of *anything* he needed right now. At least, nothing these two amazing men didn't already have about their person ... 'Yes. It won't take a minute.'

He'd just remembered where he'd put his strigil. And a whole bunch of bottles of oil.

The Kennel Club
by John Connor

Mickey Gulliver and I had been friends since our schooldays together, but once we had left university back in 1926 we seemed to go our own separate ways for several years. Best wills in the world, and all that, but almost everyone I know admits to having lost contact with classmates, as one does.

Mind you, Mickey had always been one of those reckless and daring, devil-may-care kind of guys. He was the sort who seemed to be willing and eager to experience anything and everything, and then often risk it all on the flip of a coin. Whereas I was what you would call the bookish studier – the scholar who was more usually to be found in the libraries or the lecture halls rather than in the city's pubs and clubs.

He also seemed to have more than his fair share of luck at the time, because come the finals, he walked away with a First without even appearing to break into a sweat about it.

Whatever, we went our own sweet ways after graduation, and I found a very successful niche in mechanical theory and design. I became involved with several American construction companies and got into the hydro-electrical business which had become quite the fashion back then. Did quite well for myself, I have to admit, and what with the work and the travel not being conducive to class reunions, I had completely forgotten about Mickey.

That was until I finally met up with him again, in Paris, at the 1929 International Engineering and Business Convention. He was involved with some backers who were looking to invest heavily in South America and Southern Africa. Sort of following on behind Cecil Rhodes and sweeping up the financial rewards as they went. I remained sceptical in regard to the long term, but the more we chatted as we walked around the stands, the more I got to re-acquaint myself with him.

Come the end of the day, despite discovering we were still moving in the same social circles, I had discovered little which helped to dispel my original impressions, and a lot which served to re-enforce my old images of someone who lived life to the full, and far beyond in some cases.

When it came time to leave the Convention, he enquired as to where I was staying, suggesting that as an after dinner entertainment I would be more than welcome to join him at his club that evening.

To be honest, I wasn't even slightly prepared for stepping out of an evening, let alone in one such as Paris, and so I had to send out for a more appropriate suit and tie.

At 9 p.m. precisely a taxi, apparently booked in advance by Mickey himself, arrived to collect me from my hotel, and a short drive later deposited me in an unfamiliar part of the Old Quarter. My French not being what it once was, I was hard pushed to ask the driver where we were, but after following the direction of his pointing finger, I could just about make out the dim light above a large oak and wrought iron door. Still, trusting

Mickey not to see me wrong, I knocked, waited a moment, and was then ushered respectfully into what appeared to be a well-positioned Gentlemen's Club.

I presented my card to the official by the door and moments later I was dutifully shown to Mickey's private room. Although it appeared to be a touch on the small side it had an invitingly pleasant and cosy air to it, and had been done out in an eclectic mixture of old, late Victoriana dark, and the more modernistic latest from the Art Nouveau crowd. Two large leather and button club chairs were placed pointing towards a welcoming open fire, and along with what appeared to be a well-stocked drinks cabinet there were several occasional tables to hand at armchair height on which one could easily place a drinking glass, or make use of the heavy crystal ash retainers should you wish to partake of a cigar or two during the evening's discourses.

Mickey was already enjoying an after dinner cheroot, and had thoughtfully loaded two cut glass brandy balloons with a very smooth and mature vintage. If nothing else, it certainly seemed that he had done very well for himself, despite his somewhat precarious financial lifestyle.

However, not having been forewarned beforehand I might add, it was to be on that particular evening when I had my first meeting with the curious character I came to know and call Rufus – Mickey's "dog".

It was not until much, much later that I found out more about Rufus, but back then he was a very handsome young man of around twenty-five, approximately five foot, six inches tall – although I will say now that I never actually saw him standing upright all the time I knew him. He was of an athletically slim build, but not the bone-skinny, waiflike appearance some were affecting, and his straw-blond hair had been cropped short in that Teutonic style which had somehow become strangely fashionable back then. There again, I distinctly remember never hearing him utter a word, so I could only guess his nationality from such things as his seemingly even, light brown tan, that there was possibly some Italian, or Spanish – or even South American blood to be found in his family line.

That particular evening, as was always the case on subsequent visits, he was dressed in an odd short-sleeved and short-legged one-piece garment of very fine, semi-translucent black silk. From the almost invisible seams it was easy to tell it had been designed and tailored by an obvious craftsman.

The opening at the front was finished off with a great number of small gold eyelets through which a long black ribbon had been worked. It was of such a design that it laced the garment from the neck, with the ribbon travelling all the way down and around the crotch, around the buttocks and stopping just above the very base of his spine. In many respects it reminded me of pictures I had seen of the Edwardian short style bathing costumes that had been the rage at the turn of the century. Only instead of being of a loose fitting nature, this silken version clung to his body like a second, shadowy, skin. The only other item of clothing he wore was a large leather dog collar.

In keeping with his role there was a water bowl and a food dish discreetly laid out to one side of the room, from which Rufus appeared to regularly take his meals, and again, looking back on it, I have to admit I never once saw him move around that clubroom on anything other than on all fours. At least not while I was with Mickey at the club. He really had become Mickey's pet, and Mickey wasn't shy in displaying him as and when he felt like it.

But on that first evening both Mickey and I were more

intent on catching each other up with news, talking and reminiscing about mutual friends, how well they were doing – or not, as the case may be – which debutants had been recently presented – then moving deftly into little tid-bits of scandal, mainly from within my own circle of friends – those gentlemen who prefer the company of other, like-minded gentlemen, rather than the fairer sex ...

It was around about then, during a slight pause in our conversations, that I noticed Mickey had been absently patting and petting Rufus. It consisted of nothing more than just casually stroking his head and gently rubbing a hand between his shoulder blades, but after a few moments I have to admit that I found such to be exceedingly erotic. And perhaps it was down to the brandy, the seemingly intimate privacy of the room, or probably a combination of all things, but I quickly discovered that John Thomas was erect and standing to attention, regardless of my efforts to keep him asleep whilst in polite company.

Then, so help me, Rufus rolled over onto his back and I nearly choked on my brandy at the sight of what looked like one of the largest flaccid penises I have seen, even to this day, laid out along his thigh and held in place by the almost transparent silk legging. His testicles were also of a comparable and impressive size as well. And when I finally looked back up at Mickey I saw he was readily grinning like the cat who had just had a saucer of cream!

Needless to say, from that point on the conversation moved onto the subject of Rufus, and how Mickey had discovered the unique club in the first place. It transpired that Rufus had been put up as collateral for a bad gambling debt by one of his fellow card school members, apparently just one of the many ways his previous owner had treated Rufus badly – even to the point of trying to get him castrated. Which was when Mickey stepped in and offered to exchange the IOUs and outstanding markers in return for becoming his new owner.

I know, by today's standards, this kind of transaction may seem odd and arcanely barbaric, but at the time I had heard and also read reports from places such as Hamburg and Berlin, which recounted tales of far worse. Often in similar private clubs, and more often than not on stage, specifically for public consumption. Even to the point of actual public castration.

Thankfully, such was not allowed to happen to the young Rufus. In Mickey's own words: 'All that meat and no veg? Criminal, dear boy, just criminal!'

Yet, all the time this conversation was going on around him, Rufus appeared to take little or no interest – occasionally looking towards the speaker on hearing his name being mentioned, sometimes sitting up on his heels, sometimes moving on all fours to lap up water or to take a little food from the tray. Other than that he seemed to be genuinely disinterested.

However, try as I might, I couldn't help but keep dwelling on him, becoming more and more sexually aroused by his movements, his looks, and my active imagination.

It was about then that Mickey noticed my now-very-obvious erection, and with a mischievous grin suddenly said, 'Rufus, Uncle Charlie has a bone for you! Fetch it, boy! Fetch it!'

And without a pause the young man scampered up to me, parted my legs, and unbuttoned my fly with speed. With practiced ease he carefully removed my hard penis, then popped it into his mouth, clamping down on it with his lips while all the time licking and sucking on it. Believe me, in my already aroused state it took a lot of effort not to release myself there and then, I can tell you!

Half closing my eyes I relaxed back into the chair, resting my hands on the back of his head, and let him work his magic. And work it he did! Tonguing at the shaft with little flicking movements, plunging his head down – taking a fair length of me down his throat – before pulling back so that just the tip was held between his lips, and then back down again, in a very firm and steady rhythm.

After a moment or two, but without breaking his stroke, he carefully freed my balls and then started to massage them, one at a time, with his finger tips.

Never one to miss an opportunity, Mickey had moved forwards, deftly unlaced the back of the thin silk garment as far as the crotch, and was stroking the now exposed golden buttocks with an enthusiasm bordering on serious lust. From his waistcoat pocket he quickly withdrew a small round tin of Vaseline and proceeded to work some of the petroleum jelly around, and then into, the young man's rectum.

Moments later, Mickey had positioned himself directly behind Rufus, trousers down around his thighs, and his own stiff penis clearly visible even to my half-closed eyes. Placing one hand on Rufus' hip, with the other he began to rub his member around, over, and then in between the young man's buttocks. A slight, very satisfied, grunt from Mickey, and a pause and gasp from Rufus, told me that Mickey was availing himself fully of the exciting situation.

Closing my eyes again, I thought about what I had seen between Rufus' legs – imagining that long, thick penis, pulsing and throbbing with excitement in my hand. I would be able to feel it getting harder and harder as I worked on it, watching in fascination as the foreskin puckered up, and then peeled away to reveal first the moist pink tip of his cock with the glistening, sticky slit. Then more and more of the head would be revealed, until the protective skin had been rolled back completely ...

Then I thought about Mickey, and how his cock was penetrating the young man from behind, the Vaseline lubricating his passage and allowing Mickey to slide in and out, pulling his cock out so that only the tip remained poised at his entrance, and then plunging in deeply again, thinking about the way Rufus' arsehole gripped Mickey's shaft ...

And then I knew it was too much for me to hold back! Pushing my hips slightly out of the chair as I did so, I jerked and shot my ejaculation hotly into Rufus' throat! Incredibly, he managed to swallow it completely without a pause, still working on my cock with his lips and massaging my now empty balls with his fingers – until I fell back into the chair, fully drained and satisfied.

From the haze of post-orgasm pleasure I could feel Rufus being pushed against my armchair as Mickey continued to fuck him from behind. Looking over Rufus' back I could see Mickey, one hand still firmly holding onto the young man's hip, the other around and down between his legs.

Stroking and playing with that beautifully large penis and fine balls, Mickey's arm kept moving in time with his rhythmic thrusts – the pushing getting faster and faster until, with moans from Rufus and gasps from Mickey, I knew Mickey had released himself inside the young man, and that the young man, himself, had also been pleasured into coming!

At that point, I have to admit, I drifted off into a post-coital sleep, and on waking half an hour later I found I had been properly re-dressed and was alone with Mickey – Rufus, I assumed, had left to clean himself up.

As if nothing had occurred, Mickey poured me another brandy and our amicable conversation just drifted around pleasantries and chit-chat again, until I had to leave for my own hotel.

Needless to say, during my stays in Paris, I would often visit Mickey at his club, and he would generously allow me to make use of Rufus' services whenever I felt I had need of them. That was until I had to move back to America again – losing contact with Mickey Gulliver and Rufus when Europe slipped into chaotic madness again.

Surfing Down Under
by Eva Hore

Bell's Beach in Australia is the place to be when the sun is up, the surf is high and the guys are tanned and in top form. We were travelling around Victoria and our number one destination was Bell's.

The beach has high cliffs, making the way down quite dangerous but when you see those waves breaking you know it's all worthwhile. We spent a week there before the Easter Carnival opened up. The crowds and traffic were building as everyone made their way to the beaches. Surfers of all ages and sexes surged together, eager to see the big waves.

This particular day, after a night of heavy partying, I was happy to be on my own and decided to find another beach, something a bit more less public where I could relax and think. Unbeknown to me there was a nudist beach further along the coast which I accidentally stumbled upon.

Not having been to a nudc beach before I wasn't sure of what the etiquette was. I wasn't really shy and thought I'd just strip off straight away and head for a secluded area.

Ambling along I found my cock beginning to grow. I found the heat from the sun and the cool air tantalizing my flesh very stimulating. Stumbling over the sand was making me very aware that I had half a fat. My balls swayed easily enjoying their freedom.

I chuckled to myself. Who would have thought it would be such a turn-on walking along a beach? I had my sunglasses on and every now and again I'd have a quick *perv* of the other naked bodies catching rays. There were mainly heterosexual couples but I still hoped some guy might be watching me through his sunglasses.

I knew I had a good body, always had. I had the sort of torso girls always ogled. Broad shoulders, tapered waist, great six-pack, tight butt and toned legs. I biked a lot and was extremely fit.

When I finally found a secluded cove I lay down my towel and used my clothes as a cushion for my head. It felt fucking great lying under the hot sun as it burned into my flesh, in areas that hadn't seen the sun since I was about two.

I opened my legs and breathed in deeply as it warmed me. Sucking in my stomach I allowed my hand to roam across it before moving downwards towards my crotch. I rested it there while I carefully lifted my head to make sure no prying eyes were observing me.

Being naked and out in the open is awesome. I love the sea air and listening to the crashing of waves is very relaxing so with no one about I allowed any inhibitions to fall away.

With the coast clear I inched my hand down over my cock and gave it a gentle pull, squeezing hard every now and again, enjoying it swell beneath my hand.

I closed my eyes, concentrating on the sound of the surf. I imaged a guy, blond and tanned. A fair dinkum Aussie kneeling down between my open thighs.

He slowly runs his tongue gently over my balls. I barely move. Encouraged, he licks at the base of my shaft;

his tongue is flat and wet. He continues on, licking his way to the rim around my knob.

I sigh, pleasure coursing through me as I continue with my fantasy.

With his tongue still on my knob he opens his mouth further and swallows me. I open my eyes and smile down at him as he sucks, licking lightly, his eyes sparkling mischievously.

My cock throbs, his tongue, wet with saliva, sucks more purposefully and I slide in and out more easily.

I was pumping my cock, enjoying my fantasy and the next thing I knew I was ready to blow. I opened my eyes to peer about and make sure the coast was clear, that no one was about to spoil this for me.

Gasping for breath I relaxed for a second, allowing the orgasm to spurt forth, spraying my come over the sand. The jerky spasms finally subsided and I pulled the shaft hard squeezing out every last drop, my hand resting protectively over my cock while I stretched out one leg and allowed it to flop on my thigh.

Not wanting to burn my precious jewels I rolled over on my stomach. I must have dozed for a while because the heat on my back was beginning to get hot. Suddenly I froze. A hand ran itself across my butt cheeks. Gently at first and then more determined, searching around the crack before sliding further down over my hole and under to cup my balls.

His hand was cold, as though he'd only recently come out of the surf. Perhaps he was a surfer like me?

A slight chuckle had me tensing. What should I do? I didn't want to face anyone. I didn't want to be judged by someone who thought that perhaps masturbating was not something I should be doing here on a public beach. On the other hand I found it extremely erotic to be here with a stranger, right out in the open with someone who was naked too.

I tensed when a tongue slid its way up and down my crack, nice and wet over my drying skin. The fingers were now spreading my cheeks and I gasped as the sun shone warmly on my puckered hole.

A tongue was lapping at it, probing, trying to push its way in. I clenched my cheeks together and the tongue moved further down towards my balls where it licked magically, nuzzling in to drive me wild.

My cock responded by pulsating.

The hands pulled my legs apart and a body lay between them. The tongue lapped at me while thumbs pulled my cheeks open and then the tongue tried to worm its way in.

Wiggling my butt I lifted slightly upwards and the hands held onto my hips while the body moved further between my thighs. The fingers gripped into my hips and then pulled me up by them. I leaned up on my elbows my head hanging down, my balls swaying, my cock bobbing around, wanting to fuck something too. I did not want to see who was behind me but desperately wanted to continue with this erotic experience.

The body was coming closer to me when the hands came around and grabbed at my hanging balls. A murmur of approval was close to my ear and the fingers kneaded them, then weighed them in the palm of the hands, squashing them upwards to massage.

My cock was throbbing madly, pulsating as he grabbed at the shaft with his other hand and gave it a quick pull. The hand was now underneath my arse massaging my balls gently. My cock began to stiffen more and I could feel pre-come oozing out of the slit.

I sighed loudly enjoying every second. The hand

roamed upward and a quick tweaking of my nipples had them rigid. I gasped as a cock probed between my thighs banging into me, into my butt, my thighs and as I looked down and back I could just see the knob peeking out from beneath my hairy balls.

I reached down and grabbed it. I ran my finger over the tiny slit and smeared pre-come over the knob. The body was leaning into me enjoying my hands as I tugged at the knob.

Abruptly the hands moved back to my butt and pulled my cheeks apart. The knob moved along my crack and probed the puckered skin there, inching open the hole, the tip trying to penetrate.

I wiggled around, desperate now for it to enter me, for it to slip deep inside me, for my cheeks to hug it close, to keep it inside where it was warm and welcoming.

I lifted my head up causing my butt to tilt and in it slipped. I gasped, 'Hmmm … oh …. Oh yeah.'

The body had no voice. The cock said all that needed to be said as it pulsated inside me, growing harder with every thrust. I closed my eyes tight, and in my mind tried to imagine what this man must look like. With a cock like his he must be young, I thought. It was thick, hard and very firm.

The cock pushed in and out rhythmically and I pushed back with every thrust. There was a dreamlike quality to this. The whole experience was so surreal so when the hand slapped my butt hard, my eyes flew open and my mouth made an 'O'.

Now the hand was slapping harder and each time it did my cock grew. I'd never been spanked before and with every thrust I felt his balls slapping hard against mine. The fingers tightened into my flesh and the body tensed. He was coming and so was I.

The fingers were digging into my groin as they pulled me in closer. His cock slammed into me, all hard and powerful. The walls inside me contracted. I spasmed and arched as my cock exploded before me. I moaned happily as I heard a faint grunting coming from the man and then his fingers stopped pulling and he laid his fat cock on my back, his come spurting over me, his fingers smearing it before his body collapsed and sagged against mine.

Drops of perspiration fell on me and dried as quickly as they fell. I could feel his shaft began to slacken. Still on all fours the body moved from me but I stayed there like that unsure of what to do, breathing hard.

My knees began to shake and my arms began to tremble. I snuck a look over my shoulder and saw no one was there. I collapsed onto my towel shocked at what had just happened.

Later, I rose, whipped away the sperm from my back and sides where it had dribbled, the only evidence of this mysterious man and made my way back to my car. On the way, with my sunglasses perched on my nose I eyed every body laying there. No one looked at me and no one gave any evidence of being the one who'd fucked me.

I dressed in the car park still searching for my unknown lover but alas no one was there. I've gone back the last four days in a row and lain in the exact same spot, in the exact same way but he hasn't returned.

I scan the ocean looking for some hunking guy on a board, hoping he'll ride the waves in and make his way to me.

I'll keep going, watching and waiting. When he does come I'll turn around to look deep into his eyes, into his soul. I want what I had that day and now I want it every day.

Float Your Boat
by Landon Dixon

It was a great day for fishing. Well, any day's a great day for fishing, as they say. But this particular one was even better than most – because the catch of the day was my new boyfriend, Evan.

I'd met the guy at a boat show the previous weekend, and we'd hit it off immediately, our mutual love of all things hookable, jerkable, and filletable forming a strong bond right from the beginning. And one date later – DVD night, featuring *A River Runs Though I* and *Finding Nemo* – I was hooked on the guy, line and sinker and lead and float.

He was a big, rugged, outdoorsy type, with sleek, short black hair and a black moustache, a square-cut face with a prominent cleft chin and a pair of sparkling blue eyes, thick arms and legs and barrel chest. His hands were large enough to span a cookout frying pan, hairy on the outside and calloused on the inside; his chest – from what I could see peeking out of his nylon work-shirt – was thick with black fur.

And so, one week after we'd met, we were out on the water, gone fishin'. There's no better way for really communing with a guy – and nature – than getting out all alone in a small boat on the open water. Just the two of you, hands gripping rods and lines trailing away in the lake, trolling motor purring softly as it pushes you along. Perfect for conversation, and intimacy.

'They don't seem to be biting today,' Evan commented, skinning back his Zebco cap and wiping sweat off his forehead with a brawny, hairy forearm.

'Maybe we're just not using the right bait,' I mused dreamily, gazing at the hunk of man squatted down in the Lund outboard across from me. He was wearing a blue plaid shirt, his huge upper body straining the stitching, heavy thighs and legs equally testing the seam-strength of a pair of blue jeans cuffed at the bottom. The guy was loaded as bear.

My own lanky, beanpole physique was packaged up sprightly in a tight white T-shirt and a pair of jeans I'd spray-painted on at four that morning. The T-shirt read *Bait Shop Now Open*, with a red arrow pointing downward. My all-year-tan was getting another layer under the blond fuzz on my bare arms, under the warm, rising sun. The heat and the twinkling water, that big, built dude so close, making my head swim like the fishies weren't.

I decided it was time to really set my hook. I put my fishing rod down and stood up in the boat and stretched, reaching up to the clear blue sky and bending backwards, allegedly working the kinks out of my back. Hopefully, working the kinks into my fishing buddy.

The boat wobbled a little, but I kept my footing, my cock a solid pole for all to see, outlined against the front of my faded blue jeans. I pulled my shirt out of my pants and up over my head, dropped it down into the bottom of the boat, and let the smiling sun bathe my trim, blond-fuzzed torso in delicious warmth.

'Good idea,' Evan agreed, following my lead. He set his rod aside and stood up and unbuttoned his shirt, showing me a large part of what I was really fishing for.

The boat shook along with my legs. The guy was a bear, all right – a massive black bear! His pecs were humped with muscle and doused with fur, pink nipples peeking through the screening bush, a rich trail of black hair running down his stomach and into his jeans.

We stared at one another for a couple of seconds, standing there in the quivering 12-foot open boat out on the open water, the telltale tugging on Evan's discarded rod completely ignored, bigger fish to fry right in front of us. And then we were in each other's arms, kissing like we'd just come home from the sea.

The boat rocked dangerously, Evan wrapping his burly arms around me and hugging me tight, me flinging my arms around the mountain man in delight. Our bare upper bodies melded together under the glaring sun, hot skin on skin. Evan's huge hairy chest, his rigid nipples, feeling so right, so righteous against my tightened, tingling skin; his big arms crushing me, big hands clutching my back, making me moan with pleasure into his mouth.

His lips were soft and warm and searching, thick moustache tickling. We kissed hungrily, exuberantly, devouring each other's mouths, chewing on one another's lips, neither of us giving the other any slack. All out there in the open in the middle of that forest-lined lake in that aimlessly-propelling little boat.

Evan surged his thick, wet tongue into my mouth and thrashed it around. And I got my tongue jigging, entwining it with his. I riffled my fingers through his jet-black hair (on his head), his own heavy hands sliding down my bare back and into the back of my jeans as far as they would go. As we frenched with a fearsome passion, swirling our tongues together over and over.

Until I snagged Evan's flailing pleasure tool with my

teeth and sucked on it, tugged on his tongue with my lips like I was sucking his cock. Like I *wanted* to suck on that slab of meat that was pressing hard and large into my own throbbing erection, branding me with the man's heat.

I broke the luscious suction on his tongue and gave his moustache a quick lick, then dipped my head down and licked one of his nipples, then the other. He groaned, digging his blunt fingernails into the swelled tops of my butt cheeks, as I spun my talented, cherry-red tongue around first one stiffened bud and then the other. Getting all delightfully tongue-tickled and tangled in the mat of hair on his chest.

I thrust my hands into the furry mass and clutched and squeezed his mounded pecs, pulled on his fine black coat. All the while tongue-lashing his nipples, licking them harder and fuller and higher, slathering them in hot saliva until they glistened with my ardour. Before sealing my lips around one and sucking on it, swallowing nipple and fur and tugging on both.

'Yeah!' Evan growled, tilting his head back and shuddering with pleasure.

The boat rolled and pitched, but didn't capsize, puttering along at two miles per hour as my lust for the big bear raged full-speed ahead, excitedly feeling up his hard, hairy chest and sucking on his hard, rubbery nipples. Before finally dropping lower, sinking to my knees on one of the aluminium bench seats and grabbing onto Evan's belt and tearing it open. Popping the button on his jeans and yanking his zipper down, pulling the ass, leg, and cock-hugging garment down to fully expose the man.

His cock sprang up into my face like a dancing lure must look like to a ravenous fish – big and meaty and bobbing. I grabbed onto his dong, to steady it and myself, cupping his heavy, hairy sack with my other hand.

'Fuck, yeah!' he roared, grabbing onto my blond head to steady himself.

His cock pulsed in my hand, long and thick and ridged like a deep-water fishing pole. The swollen, beating shaft was as pink as the guy's nipples, sharply-defined, mushroomed hood a purple shade. And the towering bear-stud was as hairy down below as up top, balls and legs thick with growth. I stroked his rugged man-appendage, from furry base to bloated cap, squeezing and juggling his weighty balls at the same time, breathing deep of his sweaty, musky crotch-scent.

His fingernails bit into my scalp, as I lured his cock out even longer and harder with my hot, deft hand. Getting a real good feel for the guy's pulsating rod and tightened tackle box, revelling in the heat and hardness and size, the scope of the power I wielded over the dancing bear in the boat.

Then I kissed his cap, and licked his slit, sucked his hood into my mouth and quickly and briefly tugged on it. Before opening my mouth up wide and thrusting my head forward and consuming the man's thunder-cock; my nose parting his bushy pubic hairs, his knob plumbing the back of my throat.

'Jesus!' he grunted, stunned by the rapidity and depth of my sexual strike. He stared, astonished, down at me staring up at him with my big, brown, watering eyes. His cock sunk to the fur-drenched balls in the wet-hot cauldron of my mouth and throat.

I gripped his hairy, quivering ass cheeks and kept his meat locked down in the sultry confines of Davy Jones' secret locker for a good ten seconds or so, sucking pubes up my flared nostrils, packed to the gills with pulsating cock. Then I pulled back, exhaling his pent-up dick in a gush of saliva and hot, humid air. Then I deep-throated the gleaming pike again. Getting a rhythm going. Playing the gasping guy out and then reeling him back in again. Over and over, faster and faster.

'Fuck, I – I can't take any more!' he finally cried, clawing at my head, his tree-trunk hair-barked legs trembling out-of-control.

The boat wobbled in tempo to his violent shaking, my wicked sucking pressure on his animal dong wet-vaccing a dribble of semen into the back of my throat; then a burst.

'I'm coming!' Evan bellowed, almost yanking the hair out of my frantically bobbing head.

I pulled my hands off his jumping buttocks and shot them up onto his chest, grabbing onto his furry pecs and digging my fingers into the striated flesh. Pistoning my head back and forth, sailing my lips and mouth up and down the come-hard length of his cock, sucking hard and long and deep. And triumphantly, hot, salty semen spraying my throat and filling my mouth. Landing the man's load and eagerly swallowing it down.

Until the wicked aftershocks of all-out orgasm made Evan spasm so hard that the boat rolled over to one side and took on water: pitching the bear right over the side and into the lake – me on the end of his still-leaking cock joining him in the cool, blue waters.

We splashed in and sunk down a few feet. Forcing me to finally release my grip on the guy's hairy chest and hung cock, as I fought my way back to the surface.

We bobbed together in the middle of the sun-drenched lake, in the wake of our white-hot lust, watching Evan's outboard slowly sail away. And a Ministry of Natural Resources' launch suddenly sped our way.

'Dammit!' I gasped, spitting out and treading water.

'Hey, don't sweat it,' Evan said, grinning lovingly at

me, his black hair plastered to his head, and shoulders. 'We'll get the boat back.'

'It's not that,' I spluttered. 'I don't have a fishing licence!'

The conservation officer fished us out of the water and into his boat, a 25-foot Sportcraft, sporting a whole lot more stability, room, and power than Evan's simple pleasure craft. The name tag on the man's broad chest read, *Officer Sugg,* a big, burly guy with a shaved skull, cement-mixer face, and pair of hard, brown eyes. His powerhouse arms and legs on display in his stretched-tight khaki tunic and olive shorts were every bit as hairy as Evan's (except the hair was brown in colour).

And it turned out that I didn't have to worry about Mother Nature's enforcer checking up on my fishing credentials, because the hard-man was too busy checking up on Evan's physique – with his hands – and Evan's tonsils – with his tongue. The two massive bears embracing and kissing and frenching like they were greeting each other for the first time after a long hibernation.

'Greg, this is Brendan – the fishing fanatic with the bear hunting fetish I was telling you about,' Evan said, by way of introducing me to his "friend". 'Brendan, Greg. He and I used to share a cabin on this lake.'

'Among other things, I see,' I commented dryly, folding my dripping arms over my dripping chest.

'Hey, you aren't mad, are you?' Evan said, throwing a beefy arm around Greg's cinder-block shoulders. He looked at his fur buddy and winked. 'Maybe we can cheer him up, huh, Greg?'

The brown bear flashed a row of sharp, white teeth. And then the two muscle-studs quickly stripped away their skimpy clothing, heavy-handedly helped me off with my sopping jeans and Jockeys. We all exchanged a three-way kiss by way of real introduction, our tongues flapping, my eyes straining to take in the horny guys' hard, hairy bodies. Greg was built very similar to Evan, only a little taller and a lot tanner, and even more furry. His uncut cock hung huge and gung-ho from a nest of brownish-red pubes.

They double-teamed me: Evan in front, roughly feeling up my tingling chest while he kissed me, a hand straying down to grip and squeeze my jutting cock, sending a shower of sparks all through me; Greg in behind, paws mauling my shimmering butt cheeks, tongue marauding up and down my neck and wetly in behind my ears.

'Look out!' Greg suddenly yelled, almost blowing the top of my spinning head off, pointing to starboard.

There was another boat slowly trolling our way, the waters taking on more fishers as the sun rose higher and hotter in the sky. This craft's cargo consisted of a pair of fat guys and two little kids, not 100 yards away, and closing leisurely.

'We'd better take things down to the waterline,' Greg suggested. 'This isn't family entertainment.'

He and Evan pulled me down onto the black waterproof carpeting at the bottom of the boat, so that the gunwales protected us from any prying eyes and fishy stares. And I became the meat in a bear sandwich, all three of us lying on our sides, Evan in back of me now, Greg in front – cock-to-ass-to-cock-to-ass. Resourceful Greg coming up with the necessary lubrication that got us all even more primed for anal action.

I felt Evan's swollen cockhead press in between my butt cheeks. He pushed back a cheek with one hand, fed his beefy hood into my restraining pucker with the other. I swallowed hard and tried to get loose. And the man's cap shoved through my brown-eye, his shaft gliding into my chute.

'Now you do Greg,' he gritted in my ear, his thighs pressing hotly against my trembling buttocks, meat swelling my ass with feeling.

Greg's round, rugged butt cheeks were hairy, his crack even more so, as he reached back and lifted a flap with one hand, exposing his fur-lined glory hole. I admired his ass-works briefly, before tentatively poking my hood at his opening. Then clenching my teeth and pushing forward and popping his hairy ring, plunging into the man's hot, tight, gripping bung; careful not to dislodge Evan's cock from my ass. Greg pushed backwards, putting me balls-deep and boiling in his tendril-topped chute, loaded with bear.

We started rocking together, rocking that drifting launch together, cocking each other's anuses. Evan pumping my stretched-out chute with sensual, measured strokes, as I plundered his buddy's butt to the same beat. The feeling was exquisite, fucking that fine ass, hairs stroking my shaft almost as sweetly as the man's silken chute walls; my own bung getting stoked to burning by Evan's fiery poker. I grabbed onto Greg's hairy chest and fondled his pumped-up pecs, strummed his hardened nipples, Evan's caressing and clutching hands all over my downy chest.

'Your friend knows how to dish it out,' Greg groaned, pulling on his prong.

'You're telling me,' Evan rasped in my ear, pumping my ass.

I wasn't fishing for compliments, but I took them. Churning my cock back and forth in Greg's big furry ass, erotically hemmed in on both sides, inside and out, by those two wonderfully playful bears.

Evan increased the tempo, and I picked up the pace, the pair of us sawing our cocks in and out of anuses faster and faster, with more purpose. Greg moaning and fisting his prick, getting shunted to and fro by the power of my plunger, the even more powerful thrusting of his buddy up my backside.

The boat pitched and yawed like we'd hit a squall – a storm of sexual frenzy. The sun and the fun bathing our humping bodies in sweat, greasing the frantic action even more, our breath coming in ragged gasps. The smacking sounds of hot flesh against flesh, the sucking sounds of hard cocks slamming bungs, filled the overheated air and rolled across the placid waters.

'Oh ... fuck!' Greg yelled, the first to come. His bristling body jerked in my arms, on the end of my pistoning dick, as he jacked ropes of sperm out of his cranked cock.

'Unnh!' Evan grunted, wildly pumping my ass, splashing sizzling jizz up against my bowels.

It was all too much for this pocket fisherman to withstand. The line on my sexual control snapped and my thrusting cock let loose, exploding in the superheated vice of Greg's ass and blasting the bear full of my juice. Over and over, the three of us flopping around on the bottom of the boat like gaffed fish, orgasm frying the lot of us.

Unfortunately, I had to throw Evan overboard, toss him back into the teeming ocean of men. I'm a sucker for bears, all right, but I do prefer monogamy in my wild life relationships.

He called me a couple of times, but I wouldn't take the bait. And eventually, he just had to call me the one that got away!

Beach Challenge
by Elizabeth Coldwell

I'm halfway along the beach before I hear the sound of running footsteps behind me. Putting on an extra burst of speed, even though my side aches and my lungs are burning, I still reckon I can get to the far end of the bay before them. For a moment, the moon comes out from behind a cloud. Glancing round, I see them; two shadowy figures splashing through the surf. I don't think they're actually gaining on me, but it's difficult to tell in this light.

The towel around my waist slips a little, and I hitch it up. I'd like to stop and tie it more securely, but I don't have the time. Not if I want to get away from my pursuers. I have no idea what they might do to me if they catch me.

I've found myself in some strange positions in my time, but never anything like this, sprinting along a deserted beach wearing nothing but a fluffy white towel and a pair of scuffed old training shoes. I suppose it'll make a good story to tell when I get back to London. But London seems so far away at this moment.

I stumble over a pebble the size of my fist, manage to keep from falling over entirely, and head for the gently zig-zagging path that leads up the cliff and back to the house. So close now, so close ...

And then I feel a hand grab my bare thigh and I go

sprawling in the sand. There's a triumphant, mocking laugh as I lie there, winded. I close my eyes and wonder what my forfeit will be.

When Jeff invites me to his stag night, I know it's going to involve something exotic. After all, the days of hiring a room over a pub and a peroxide stripper dressed as a policewoman, who'll rub her tits in the groom's face to the delight of his leering mates, are long gone. Now it's a weekend in Prague or Tallinn or wherever the pound's strong and the beer is cheap. A bloke who used to work in our sales department claimed when his old boss got married, he took his three best salesmen, him included, to Amsterdam and paid for them all to have sex with whichever of the window girls took their fancy.

Fun as that may sound, I hope Jeff isn't planning anything too expensive: we might have been mates for eight years, since we first met at university, but I've never moved in the same exalted financial circles as him and the rest of his close friends and never will.

Fortunately, it turns out one of those friends, Reuben – who is also going to be Jeff's best man – belongs to a family which appears to own a considerable chunk of Cornwall. His old man's going to be away on business in Hong Kong for a couple of weeks, which means we'll have the run of his house for the weekend. Actually, the way Jeff describes it, it sounds more like a country seat than a humble house. All I know is it means sorting out a cheap rail fare to Liskeard, then Reuben will pick me up at the station. No need for a passport, no queuing for hours at Heathrow, no cut-price airfare that actually ends up costing you a fortune once they've added on the cost of checking in, stowing your baggage and selling you an in-flight sandwich. Just sun, sea and the contents of

Reuben's dad's drinks cabinet. My idea of bliss.

Reuben is waiting for me at Liskeard station when the train pulls in. He and Jeff became best friends at boarding school, but when Jeff went to university, Reuben spent a year backpacking round Australia and the Far East before getting a job with an investment bank. So far, so much the stereotype. But as he hefts my rucksack into the boot of his sporty little Mini and flashes me a broad smile, I find myself unexpectedly warming to him. He has the lean, athletic build of a surfer – which is, apparently, how he spends most of his weekends, riding the waves off the Cornish coast – and dark, floppy hair which he brushes out of his eyes as he talks.

Reuben drives fast and a little recklessly, as only someone who is completely familiar with these twisting high-hedged country roads could feel confident in doing. He's blasting out heavy rock music over the Mini's speakers, raising his voice to ask me questions over the rumbling beat.

'Jeff tells me you're a teacher?' he says, twisting slightly in his seat to address me.

'Yeah, that's right,' I reply, wishing he'd keep those surprisingly long-lashed hazel eyes of his on the road. 'A-level Spanish. Not particularly glamorous.'

'But necessary. All I can manage in Spanish is *"una cerveza, por favor"*. I try and make it a rule that wherever I am in the world, I know how to order beer.' He laughs. 'Now all I need to learn is how to say, "Fancy a fuck?" and I've got it sorted.'

I'm about to enlighten him, but he takes a sharp right, pulling the car up in front of a set of heavy iron security gates. He gets out of the car for long enough to punch in the code that opens the gates, then hops back in and guns the Mini up a drive which is easily half a mile in length.

The house at the end of it looks like something my parents, who are both card-carrying members of the National Trust, pay money to traipse round every summer. I try not to let my jaw drop. This really is how the other half live.

'Am I the last to arrive?' I ask, as Reuben presents me with my luggage.

'Not quite,' he replies. 'Craig's still on his way over from Bristol. I got a text from him to say the traffic on the A38's murder.' He slams the boot shut. 'But then it is Friday night, what does he expect? Everyone else is getting ready for dinner. Come on, I'll show you to your room.'

It's another 40 minutes before the errant Craig arrives, flustered and apologising for his lateness. The rest of us are lounging in the antique-strewn living room, glugging beer and getting to know each other a little better if we don't already. Dinner's almost ready, so Craig dumps his bag and comes to join us.

After a meal of coq au vin and crusty French bread, prepared by Reuben's father's housekeeper before she left for the weekend, we retire to the drawing room. This is all so alien to me – housekeepers and drawing rooms aren't exactly commonplace in the suburb of Sheffield where I grew up – but I somehow feel relaxed in this environment. Perhaps it's the fact Reuben is so welcoming. More likely, it's the excellent Burgundy he's been plying us with throughout dinner. Whatever, Jeff and I have fallen back into our old, easy groove of friendship and I'm starting to feel comfortable with his other friends, too.

Which is when Reuben suggests we start doing tequila shots. He insists on drinking it in what he calls "the traditional way": lick salt off the back of your hand; down the tequila; then bite on a slice of lime. It's hardly my favourite drink – I find the oily texture of the liqueur slightly off-putting – but the mood I'm in I'm game for anything. A couple of shots apiece drains the bottle.

'And you know what that means,' Reuben says, clutching the empty bottle. 'It's time for a little game.'

He grabs a sheet of paper, starts tearing off strips and scribbling on them as we watch. The strips he folds and places in an empty ice bucket.

'OK. We're going to play *spin the bottle*. I'll take the first spin. Whoever it points at has to take one of those slips. Some of them are questions, some of them are challenges. You just have to do whatever the paper says. If you refuse, or if you get a challenge and fail it, then you have to pay a forfeit.'

It sounds straightforward enough. Reuben's spin leaves the bottle pointing at Craig. We quickly learn the sort of question Reuben has in mind for us all to answer when Craig finds himself having to tell us how he lost his virginity. There's no hesitation, no flush of embarrassment at having to reveal something so personal. Instead, Craig launches into the story of how, on the night of his 18th birthday, he was seduced by one of his mother's friends, who came to deliver him a present. He smiles at the memory. 'It was only when Helen followed me into my bedroom and undid her coat so I could see that all she had on underneath it was her stockings and suspenders that I twigged what kind of present it was.'

Craig describes the incident in vivid detail, remembering how it felt to be smothered in Helen's warm tit-flesh as she pressed her nipple into his sucking mouth and how she straddled his groin, sinking down on his straining cock till he was buried to the root in her wet, clutching pussy hole. I look round the room. It's hard to tell for sure in the soft firelight, but Jeff seems to be shifting his position, as though his chinos are suddenly too tight for him, and I could swear a couple of the other lads have got prominent bulges in their pants.

When Craig finally finishes his tale, he gives the bottle a spin. The next victim is one of Jeff's City mates, Alan. He unfurls the paper and reads aloud, 'Have you ever sucked another man's cock?'

It seems like an outrageous question from where I'm sitting, but Alan just snorts and replies, 'Come on, who hasn't?'

Speak for yourself, I think, but he's already admitting how it happened. 'In my first year at halls, I shared a room with a lad called Darryl. Nice lad, on the university football team, parents from Antigua originally, if I remember. One night, we both had too much to drink and I ended up telling him I'd never really seen a black cock before and, you know, was it true they're all massive? I thought I'd offended him, but he just laughed and invited me to take a look. Well ...' Reuben has opened another bottle of wine by now, and Alan encourages him to top up his glass. '... A look turned into a feel, turned into a taste ... He wasn't any bigger than me, to be honest, so that one bites the dust, but I'll never forget how he felt in my mouth. Hot and vital. And the taste of his spunk, slipping down my throat ...'

A soft groan from somewhere to my right tells me at least one person here finds the story more of a turn-on than Craig's account of his seduction by a horny cougar.

Alan swallows another mouthful of Burgundy. 'I only ever tried it the once, but I'll never regret it.'

He stares thoughtfully at the empty tequila bottle, as though about to add something else, then changes his mind and spins it. It's a half-hearted effort, wobbling a couple of times before coming to rest with its snout pointing directly at me.

'Chris, dig in, mate!' Reuben invites me, pushing the burnished copper ice bucket at me. I snatch up one of the slips, and take a breath before reading it.

All it says is "Beach Challenge", which leaves me baffled.

'Ah, the Beach Challenge.' Reuben smiles evilly. 'Are you a runner, Chris?'

'Well, I go jogging after work a couple of times a week,' I admit.

'You'll be fine then,' he assures me. 'The beach is round the back of the house – don't look so surprised, all the big houses here have their own private stretch of beach. Anyway, all you have to do is run along it and get back up the cliff path before the people who'll be chasing you catch you. If you don't, then you have to pay a forfeit.'

'Is that all?' I murmur weakly. Suddenly, having to confess to some past sexual adventure doesn't seem half so bad any more.

'Well, the good news is you get a couple of minutes' head start, and I'll be kind when I choose the lads who'll be chasing you. The bad news is you have to run the course wearing nothing but a towel. Oh, and your trainers, of course. I wouldn't want you to twist your ankle on the pebbles.'

'You're joking,' I say, but it's obvious he's not. There's a little cloakroom just across the hallway, and I'm sent in there to change. I have to bring all my clothes out with me so everyone can see I haven't cheated by keeping my underwear on.

Emerging a couple of minutes later with a towel knotted securely round my waist, I feel incredibly foolish.

I can't help feeling this isn't the first time Reuben and some of the others have played this particular game.

Reuben has chosen Alan and Jeff to chase me. Alan strikes me as the least athletic of all of them, and I hope Jeff will go easy on me because we're friends. It makes having to hand Reuben my clothes, black briefs prominent on the top of the pile, just a little easier.

The four of us make our way out to the back garden and down the steps to the beach. Everyone else decides to stay where they are and make further inroads into Reuben's father's wine cellar. From the looks on a couple of faces, I wouldn't be at all surprised if they start up a game of their own in our absence. A game which involves wanking – either themselves or each other. They've all been at boarding school, after all. They've probably been playing with their cocks in front of each other since they first realised what they were for.

The June evening is surprisingly warm, and suddenly what's about to happen doesn't seem so bad. I'm fit, I can run pretty fast when I want to and, most importantly of all, I'm damned if I'm going to pay any kind of forfeit.

'OK, Chris,' Reuben says. 'You've got two minutes, then Alan and Jeff are after you. Ready ... Go!'

I can see the cliffs at the far end of the beach, and know I'll be as good as halfway across by the time the others set off. I'm going to make it, and I keep thinking that up to the point where that hand grabs my leg and brings me down hard.

Winded by the fall, I keep my head down for a moment as I recover. When I finally scramble on to my hands and knees and look up, wanting to know which of the two of them caught me, I can't believe what I see. Alan and Jeff are only just jogging up to this stretch of beach, Alan looking painfully red in his bespectacled face. Instead, it's Reuben who felled me.

'You!' I exclaim. 'But how ...?'

His expression is smug. 'You might have had a two-minute start over those two, but I set off at the same time as you did. And unlike you, I know this beach like the back of my hand.'

I should have known. There was no way Reuben was going to let me win this challenge. Here I was, thinking I'd been accepted by him, and all the time he was planning this.

'Get up,' he says, and I rise slowly to my feet. Before I can react, Reuben reaches for the knot of my towel and yanks it off me. Suddenly, I'm standing stark naked but for my trainers in front of three blokes, two of whom I've never met before tonight. Instinctively, I cup my hands over my crown jewels, but Reuben's having none of that and orders me to put my hands on my head.

Now, I feel as though I'm on display, and that thought causes something utterly unexpected to happen. My cock begins to rise, twitching and thickening as the others take in the sight of my firm arse and chest with its light sprinkling of blond hair. Alan can't seem to stop looking at my swelling erection. I've always known I'm rather bigger than average, but his eyes are bugging out of his head as he registers my true dimensions.

Reuben is twisting the towel between his hands, forming it into a thin rope, and I wonder whether he's intending to whip me with it. Isn't that what public schoolboys have always done for fun, lash each other with wet towels? And why is the thought of it causing a dark, hot stream of desire to course through my veins?

He seems to have other ideas, though. Turning to the other two, he tells them to go back to the house and run a cold bath in the first-floor bathroom, then find as much ice as they can in the kitchen and dump it in the bath. So he's going to use the towel to bind my wrists, then drag me up the cliff and throw me into the bath. Maybe the size of my cock intimidates him, and he's going to try to cut it down to size. When it's all shrivelled up by the ice, he'll invite the others in to laugh at me and …

Fuck, even the thought of being humiliated in that way is turning me on. What am I turning into? I watch Alan and Jeff pick their way through the pebbles and on to the smooth stretch of sand that leads up to the cliff path. Knowing what's coming next, I put my arms out in front of myself, hands clasped, inviting Reuben to fasten them together.

He looks at me for a long moment, then relaxes visibly. 'Thank Christ for that. I thought I'd never get rid of them.'

'Just what's going on here?' I ask. 'If you're going to tie me up and throw me in that ice bath, let's just get it over with, shall we?'

He laughs so hard at that I think he's in danger of pulling a stomach muscle. 'Throw you in the bath? Is that what you think's going to happen?' He must be able to read the anguish in my expression, because he says, 'Look, that was only an excuse to get those two out of here.'

Now I'm totally confused. And still hard. My cock continues to strain upwards even as Reuben wraps his fist round it.

'Don't you realise, Chris, I've wanted you since the moment you got in my car? I just had to find some way of getting you on your own.'

'So you bring me down to the beach, make me run a mile and then strip me bare …' I want to object further, but I can't. Reuben's grip has changed to a soft back-and-forth motion, slowly wanking me. And though I've always thought I never had any interest in men, I'm starting to realise I was wrong. This feels so good. Unlike most of the girls I've been with, who never squeeze my cock quite hard enough out of some misplaced fear they might break it, Reuben is applying just the right amount of pressure. When his thumb strums insistently over the spot just below the head, my breath catches in my throat. That's when he knows he's got me hooked.

'Feels great, doesn't it, Chris?' he murmurs. 'But it'll feel even better when my mouth takes over.'

God, he can't be talking about sucking me off, can he? My mind flashes back to Alan's tale of giving his room-mate a blowjob, his loving description of how it felt to swallow cock. But what was it like for the guy on the receiving end?

I get my answer as Reuben goes down on his knees before me, heedless of the little waves breaking around my trainer-clad feet. At first, he nuzzles his nose into my bushy curls, breathing in my musk, before his tongue snakes out to trace the wrinkled contours of my balls.

That's the moment the moon chooses to come out from behind the clouds, bathing us both in its glacial white light. I don't know what makes me glance up towards the cliff top, but when I do I'm almost sure I can see two figures silhouetted against the sky. The thought Jeff and Alan might be up there, watching as Reuben lovingly licks my balls, is almost too exciting for me to bear. Seems that below my seemingly vanilla exterior, there lurks a shameless exhibitionist who gets off on being played with for the benefit of a watching audience, and I'm more than happy for Reuben to exploit this new-found knowledge.

At last, he stops teasing me and I feel his hot lips engulf the head of my cock. My knees almost buckle and I fight to stay steady on the shingle. Reuben can't swallow too much of my length, but he does his best, my helmet butting hard against the roof of his mouth in my excitement. As this is all so new to me, I let him set his own pace, even though I'm struck with the urge to really fuck his mouth.

His fingers are slick with my pre-come and his saliva where they dribble over his hand, and suddenly one of those fingers is pressing at the entrance to my arse. While I'm no stranger to getting my cock sucked, no one has ever tried to penetrate me, and I tense against the intrusion.

'Relax,' Reuben says, letting my cock drop from between his lips. His dark eyes are soft and wet as he looks up at me, inviting my trust. He'll stop if I demand it, I know that, but as his finger seeks entry again, I go with my instincts and unclench my muscles. That wet finger gradually pushing into me is opening me up to a whole new dark realm of pleasure – not just physically, but mentally, too. As his mouth keeps sucking and his finger keeps probing, I find myself wondering what it would be like to take something larger back there.

Reuben must realise what I'm thinking, because he stops sucking me and growls, 'I'm going to have your arse now.'

The moon has disappeared again, and I can no longer tell whether there's anyone up on the cliff, watching. I'm sure they're still there, waiting for the climax of the performance. The moment when Reuben's cock plugs my virgin arse.

He strips out of jeans that are wet from where he's been kneeling in the surf. He's not wearing anything beneath them, and his dick rises up as though celebrating being free in the night air. It's shorter than mine, with a slim, tapered head. Not the monster I'd been simultaneously hoping and fearing to see, though I still can't help wondering how it's all going to fit inside me. Not bothering to remove his rugby shirt, he unfurls my discarded towel and spreads it on a smooth patch of sand.

'On all fours,' he orders me, gesturing to the towel. I respond more strongly when he starts taking control, and I hurry to obey, feeling the sand yield slightly beneath the pressure of my palms and kneecaps.

At first, Reuben does nothing. I don't look up, but I'm sure he's taking the time to study the way I look, rump raised and inviting. Then I hear him spit, and feel something trickling down the crack of my arse. It's the filthiest thing anyone has ever done to me, and my cock twitches of its own volition.

Reuben comes close behind me, and I feel him plant a soft kiss on each of my cheeks. 'Gorgeous – and all mine,' he says, then something hot and hard is nudging at my arsehole. As he instructed me before, I do my best to relax, feeling certain there's no way something that big is going to be able to enter me. Then the muscle yields and he's inside. There's a sharp sting as he pushes deeper, but I fight against the discomfort and gradually something sweeter and more welcome replaces it.

Again, I let Reuben move at his own pace, his lean, semi-clad body covering mine as he begins to move. Slowly at first, letting me get used to the way his rigid cock fills me so wonderfully, then harder and more forcefully till his balls are really slapping against my arse with every stroke. As he fucks me, he reaches round and grabs my hard-on. I think I'll lose my load the moment his fingers touch me, but somehow I hold back.

Everything that is happening is so novel, so amazing that even with all my willpower it takes just a few more ruthless thrusts, a few more strokes of those clever fingers and my spunk is spilling out. Creamy drops spatter over the soft white towelling beneath me. My arse clutches tight around Reuben's shaft as my pleasure crests, triggering his own explosion deep in my bowels.

We roll over on the sand, spent and sweating. I push his damp, dark hair out of his eyes and our lips meet in a long, glorious kiss. After the ferocity of our fucking, these slow, tender embraces are all the more satisfying.

Reuben only stops caressing me when he sees me doing my best to stifle a yawn. I'm succumbing to a combination of good wine and even better sex, and desperately ready for my bed.

'OK, I suppose that's enough for one night,' he says. 'Let's get some sleep and in the morning you can show me just how well you suck cock.'

That'll be another new experience for me, but as we walk off the beach with our arms round each other I have no qualms about trying it. It doesn't matter what challenge Reuben sets me from now on; I know I'm going to be more than capable of rising to it.

A Birthday Present
by Ruth Ramsden

The smell is the first thing you notice: The soft, slightly sweet smell of incense bruising the air, hinting at spice and wood and other hidden oils. But there is something else more exciting, more familiar – a ribbon of cold astringency running through the air in the warmth beyond the entrance and you strain your eyes through the gloom to try and see. This is what you wanted and I am waiting for you.

I have lit only candles and they make vivid pools in the darkness beyond the door. I don't want you to be familiar with the room, with the things I've done. I don't want you to see everything here. Just now, I don't want you to see anything at all. As you step towards the threshold I tell you to stop. You try to look around.

'Stay where you are.' I say firmly, 'Close your eyes.' Your shoulders tense and you look down, closing your eyes, doing as you are told. You will have to trust me. You are already feeling nervous and a little afraid.

I can see the tumble of dark curls around your forehead and the fan of eyelashes on your cheek. You can sense me as I come to you and your breathing becomes shallower. I like the way your head is bowed and your arms are loose by your sides. You jump slightly as I touch your back, which is satisfying but I need you to be a little calmer than that. I spread my fingers out, running them down your spine, pushing the nails inwards. You can feel them dig into the skin through your clothing and you steady yourself against them. Good. I stretch out my hand on your shoulders, enjoying the feel of the taut muscles swelling into your neck, the stillness of your torso.

You can feel my warm breath on your face now. You swallow. You want to look. I push my hand up into your hair, spoiling nature, holding it tightly, taking pleasure in your intake of breath. You feel how it pulls and you frown against the pain.

Then I force your face down into the thing I hold in my other hand. There is a sudden small panic of brief suffocation and, as you breathe in, the nature of that other familiar scent becomes clear. Latex. That slightly chocolate pungency, a bitter, natural aromatic – and your body reacts. It reacts the way it has always done to the smell and the cold, smooth, thick, resilient skin. You can feel your cock swell and harden.

'Stay still,' I say, 'Keep your eyes closed.' I offer up the object and you nuzzle into it as I reach down between your legs to feel the growing bulge. You push your hips against the spread of my fingers.

'I said stay still.'

You stand up straighter, with an affecting shiver and I take the rubber object and unzip it. It is a hood. You start to tremble in anticipation when you realise and I fit it over your head and zip up the back, making sure it is snug and that you can breathe adequately from the nose, as I zip up the eyes and mouth. You can smell it. You can taste it. It caresses your skin with its hard fragrance and with its silky, oily essence.

Since childhood this has been your fantasy, the delight that accompanied your first sticky fumblings into adulthood and beyond; the shame that you tried to hide, strike out of your life so many times but which has always returned with renewed sweetness, reminding you of the exaltation and ascendancy of sex.

I take your hand and lead you into the room, and the soles of your feet steady you on the smooth surface I have created, the sheets of rubber that clothe the small space all around to the walls. I listen with satisfaction to your grunt of surprise beneath the mask.

You can feel my fingers loosen the belt of your jeans, undo, unzip, pull down, undress. Your erection is now straining against the material of your underwear. It's almost uncomfortable in its confinement and it amuses me briefly to see fabric so tortured. I help them off and down. Naked from the waist down, I now strip you completely, letting your shirt slide away on the smooth flooring.

You are my creature now, standing in the middle of the half light of the room, waiting. You are hot, aware of your arousal, slightly humiliated by the ease of this excitement, made vulnerable by your nakedness and cut off from sensation by the pungent confinement of the hood. You can feel your heart-rate quicken and anticipation floods your mouth with saliva like the expectation in hunger of a favourite meal. I promised you this. And you have absolutely no idea what is going to happen next.

I leave you standing there for a moment and admire you. The mask cuts off your identity but this makes you my special thing. Something only I am allowed to know. I can see your chest move with a slight panic that you are controlling and enjoying. Your shoulders are tense but your arms loose. Your legs slightly parted, nicely shaped and muscular. And the most vivid thing about you – your cock is huge and hard, almost a separate living creature that makes an obvious demand, despite your submission. I decide on something punitive.

'Slut! Look at you, stood there ... I can smell you, whore!'

You hear me and hang your head, you can feel the blush of embarrassment prickle across your skin momentarily. You want to say something emolliating, apologetic, pacifying. But the fear that prompts this contrition is too exciting.

'You know what happens to sluts, don't you?'

You nod your head, even though you have no clue.

The arm binders are rubber. Their straps are rubber and the buckles shiny stainless steel. They are heavy and cold and I pull your arms back; you moan slightly as I strap you into them, feeling the weight and the new tension in your shoulders. I brush my hands lightly over your chest and up to your neck as you steady yourself, breathing heavily.

For the first time you realise how difficult this is going to be. The posture collar is thick rubber, of course it is, and encloses your neck in a high, uncomfortable stranglehold forcing your head up and back, a tortuous counterpoint to the binders. It has a single, thick steel ring at the front.

But this is going to get worse. A sheen of perspiration blossoms across your chest as you start to labour a little beneath the hood and you hear a faint click and a tug as I attach the trigger hook on the rope to the ring in your collar. Your feet leave sweaty marks on the latex sheet as I lead you to the centre of the room.

You can feel the arm binders cutting into the skin under your arms, becoming uncomfortable and sore and you can feel the tingle in your fingers as your circulation struggles with the restriction. You keep your eyes closed under the hood as the sweat slicking down your hair will sting your eyes and you can taste the salt in your mouth.

This is hard. Very hard. I leave you to stand and steady yourself while I watch you, a tortured object in my rubber room. In this dark dungeon, the rope attached to your collar snakes up from the fitful light of the candles into the gloom of the ceiling and the pulley safely secured there.

I go to where the other end of the rope is tied off against the wall and watch you with satisfaction as I begin to pull. I can hear your muffled cry as the rope takes up the slack and urges your body forwards and up. You look beautiful, struggling with panic, stepping and sliding on your tiptoes on the greasy surface beneath you. I can hear you moaning.

I raise my arm back quite high. At the first hard slap on your arse your whole body jumps forward, your feet stepping and slipping, trying to gain purchase as you swing and I hear your muffled yelp through the secure enclosure of the hood. I can hear your agonised breathing. You manage to steady yourself. I hit you again. A groan. Again. I spank your beautiful bottom, your tight little arse, until your legs shake from the effort of trying to stay upright and each cheek is a glowing fiery red, until my hand stings abominably. You are moaning continually, a slow exhausted noise and I unzip the mouth on the hood and hear your grateful gasp of air.

'Slut! You enjoyed that!'

You have no hope of denying this. Your cock is hard and tense and you ache inside, a much more urgent feeling than the sting that still warms your arse cheeks or the strain in your neck and arms. To make this point, I push a ball gag into your mouth and buckle it viciously behind your head. I pull on a pair of tight surgical gloves and watch your chest move, struggling to draw in air behind the gag as I pour lube into my cupped hands, sliding it smoothly over the latex skin. From behind I push my fingers between your legs, hard and begin to finger you, just behind your balls, pressing, massaging. Then you feel the sensation shudder through you as I slide a finger inside your arse, holding you in space, my other hand on your belly. I can hear you whimpering as I insert another finger, then another, pushing and stretching you. I can feel you shaking – the throbbing of your cock, the profound sensation at the tips of my exploring fingers and the spiteful glow of your arse are confusing, mind-numbing, liberating.

I reach between your legs again and feel your balls, letting my lubed latex fingers slide over them as I grasp and squeeze, and you swallow noisily in your throat and groan as I move my fingers inside you, exciting that most delicate spot. My slippery fingers move again, parting your arse wider, pushing all the way into you, one, two, three, four fingers and the rest and I take sweet delight at hearing you cry out, a muffled squeal behind the gag, as I fist you.

Each slow thrust inside you brings you on more; your breath is coming in short, shallow gasps and you grunt with each deep stroke. You have forgotten that you have any other existence than this moment, than feeling me inside you and I am smiling, smiling because I can hear your anticipation.

I reach around your thighs and, as I thrust into you again, I grab your cock with my other gloved hand. I can feel it hard and warm through the latex, and the thick pre-come oozes urgently as I spread it round the head of your cock. You are suspended in rubber by my hands, it's all you can see and all you can taste and all you can feel beneath your feet. You cannot breathe behind the gag.

Spit flecks the rubber of your mask as you struggle and dance in the support of my arms. I can feel you strain for air and release as I start to stroke your cock with my rubber fingers, slowly at first, then faster, the counterpoint to my fist. All I have to do is squeeze now you are on the brink of suffocation, on the very edge of drowning in the soft substance of that pungent, elastic second skin. I move my hand faster. The dark beckons you through the pain in your chest and the ache in your jaws.

'Slut!'

Can you even hear me now? Does it even matter? Your whole body shakes convulsively as you cry out from behind the gag, a delicious sound torn from deep inside you and your cock suddenly jerks and throbs as you come hard and helplessly, the warm stream spurting again and again over my fingers.

I remove the gag and listen to the grateful gasps filling your lungs again with air. You are only barely aware when I withdraw my hand from you, unbuckle the binders and collar.

Finally, I remove your hood and your legs buckle. Your body is soaked, your jaw slack and although your eyes are half closed I can see in the shadows that the pupils are just pin pricks. The warmth of the room has enclosed you, the candles are fainter and the only sound is of your breathing, now long soft breaths like sleep. The sweat on your body is drying and you ache.

I hold you and you curl up in my arms like a child. You are smiling faintly and I am happy. I haven't finished with you yet. There is still the small matter of *my* satisfaction. After all, this is my birthday, not yours.

The Anniversary Gift
by Garland

The full pillows were behind me. I was sinking into them
like a ship sinking into the waves. There were six of them
propping me up. My legs were spread wide and except for
the cowboy hat perched crookedly on my head I was
nude. My dick was semi-hard. I lightly stroked it wishing
it would grow harder as I watched Sug slowly strip in
front of me. He was still wearing his suit.

Slowly like a curtain being opened to reveal the star he
unbuttoned his shirt and let it slide down his broad
shoulders revealing his pecs and dark curly hair. His tie
hung in between his pecs. Smiling he rubbed it over his
chest and nipples before unbuttoning his pants and
stepping out of them and his briefs. He was hard. Sug was
always hard. Just mention the word sex and his dick
sprung to life.

'Like what you see?' he asked.

'You know I do, Sug,' I answered.

'You don't look like you do,' he said indicating my
now flaccid penis.

'Come on, Sug,' I said. 'You know that don't mean
nothin'.'

'I do know one thing,' he said confidently as he
walked toward me.

'What's that?'

'That I love a man with an accent,' he said before kissing me.

Sug told everyone that my Texas accent, made husky thanks to years of heavy chain-smoking, was what made him fall in love with me. Sug had moved to our small town from Seattle. According to him no one had a real accent up there.

'Still nothing?' He asked looking down at my penis and breaking me out of my thoughts.

'I'm sorry, Sug. You know how much I love you and your body.'

'Let's see if I can get you hard,' Sug said burying his face in-between my legs. Sucking and stroking he pulled everything out of his bag of tricks, even hitting his hard cock against mine, but it was useless. I just couldn't get hard.

'I'm sorry, Sug.' I repeated what had become the catchphrase of this lovemaking session as I flopped back onto the pillow. Taking out a cigarette I lit up and inhaled deeply, closing my eyes in bliss.

'What's wrong?' Sug asked lying next to me. 'It's Wednesday. Hump day.'

'It's Wednesday. Hump day,' I answered, eyes still closed.

'What are you talking about?'

I opened my eyes and gazed deeply into his dark honey eyes. 'Our lives have become routine. Day in and day out. You go to the office. I stay home and write. On the weekends we go hunting or fishing or camping. Wednesdays we make love right after dinner.'

'Are you saying you're bored with me, Huston?' Sug asked, eyes full of hurt.

'No. Of course not! It's just … I don't know. I need some variety in my life. In our life. In our sex life. We even have sex the same. You strip except for the tie. I wear my cowboy hat: we do the 69; then doggy; then missionary; then cowboy. The only time I get any variety is when I write erotica. It's only natural, Sug,' I assured him, stroking his hair and trying not to bruise his fragile male ego. 'These things happen. We've been together ever since we were sophomores in high school. That's almost 15 years. Naturally we're goin' to fall into routines.'

He looked away hurt. Sighing I inhaled deeply and savoured the smoke tickling my lungs before exhaling. We laid there, side by side, in silence. Sug was staring intently at the virginal white wall; I thought he was going to burn a hole through it.

I stared at the man I had been with since I was 15 years old. When had he become a man? It seemed like only yesterday he was a teenager and we were ready to take the world by the ass. He was going to be a lawyer who stuck up for the little guy and got rid of corruption and I was going to change the world with my writing. That seemed so long ago yet just like yesterday.

I did love him. He was the only man I had ever loved. The only man I had ever been with. He still had a great body compliments of a rigorous seven-day-a-week workout schedule he kept religiously. In rain or shine, sickness or health, Sug worked out. His chest was still solid and his stomach flat. His hair was just beginning to lighten and I noticed a touch of silver at the temples that gave him a distinguished look.

'Sug,' I spoke gently and laid a hand on his beating heart. 'Please, don't take this personally.'

'Are you giving me the, we-need-to-take-some-time-apart, speech?' he asked, still not looking at me.

'Sug, I swear you should have been an actor the way

you turn everything into such a heavy drama. Of course I don't think we need some time apart. I think we need to spice things up a little.'

Finally, he turned toward me. His eyes were sparkling like fresh cut diamonds.

'Now, Sug, don't start crying. There's nothing to cry about.'

'You'd cry too, Huston, if you couldn't turn on the man you loved.'

'You know you turn me on. We just need to find a different way to turn me on,' I said stroking his cheek.

'You think we can?'

'I write erotica for a living,' I said, winking at him before stubbing out my cigarette. 'I think I can come up with something. After all, I am known as The King Of Gay Erotica.'

He smiled and we kissed. Placing the cowboy hat on him I looked down at his still hard penis.

'Hate to waste a good boner.' I smiled at him and slowly snaked my way down his hard body.

Looking up at him I massaged his curly black pubic hair. My hands got lost in his dark nest. Sucking on his balls I ran my hand up and down his hard length. We never took our eyes off each other. Slowly I licked his penis like an ice cream cone in July before opening my mouth wide and engulfing him. My hands explored his chest, pinching his nipples and getting lost in his chest hair as my head bobbed up and down. Flicking my tongue against the head of his dick like a snake I lapped up the little bits of pre-come that had leaked out.

'Get up,' I told him. 'Stand at the edge of the bed.'

Laying down I looked up at his hard penis, glistening with my spit. Cupping his balls in my hand I kissed and sucked on them before licking that sensitive place right between a man's balls and asshole. Sug's knees buckled and his body shuddered. Opening my mouth he guided his penis in and vigorously pumped in and out. The tip of his penis tickled my tonsils. Smiling I massaged his balls. His moans were music to my ears. Thank God I didn't have a gag reflex.

Hoisting me up our lips joined. Sug's tongue licked my lips before penetrating my mouth. Our tongues swirled around each other, flicking together. Our hands roamed each other's body, leaving nothing unexplored as we tried to make everything old and familiar new and exciting.

Wrapping my legs around him and clinging tightly to his back I kissed his broad shoulders and nibbled on his earlobe as he slid his penis inside me. Moaning in sync we kissed deeply as we made love. We had never had sex in the standing position before! He was able to penetrate me so much deeper and give every one of my erogenous zones equal attention. I loved it and couldn't believe we hadn't thought of this before. My penis, now hard, thank God, was pressed in between us like rose petals pressed between the pages of a memory book. My stomach quivered and I felt that familiar tingle start way down in my toes and pulsate all through my body as I came, staining our chests with my come. Seconds later Sug exploded deep inside me with a low groan.

'How's that for charging things up?' he asked me as we lay in bed, his eyes drooping like a wilted rose and his voice groggy with sleep. Sug always fell asleep after we made love.

'It's a start,' I whispered enjoying my post-coital cigarette.

Before long Sug's chest was rising and falling rhythmically and I was alone with just my thoughts and the warm glow of my cigarette for company. Sug had fulfilled my request to try something different with our love making so why did I still feel so incomplete?

Slipping on a pair of sweats and a T-shirt I tiptoed downstairs and sought sanctuary in my office. Lighting up another cigarette I continued working on a project I had started months ago but just couldn't commit to finishing. It was about two boyfriends who, finding their relationship has become stale, seek out a young guy to help them spruce things up a bit. It was good and very hot. But I could only work on it for a few minutes before I got so frustrated I wanted to scream.

Pacing back and forth in the suddenly claustrophobic office I tried to will myself to finish the damn thing. It would be my hottest novel yet.

By the time the sun had stained the blue black sky a magnificent blood orange colour I had smoked a whole pack of cigarettes. I stared at my computer. I had just gotten to the part where my protagonists enlist the help of an 18-year-old hustler. Reading and rereading what I had, my eyes slowly grew wide. Maybe I had a solution to the problem between Sug and I.

'Have you been here all night?' His voice made me jump. 'Sorry,' he said. 'Didn't mean to scare you.'

'You didn't,' I said truly smiling at him. 'I was just thinking.'

'About what?' he asked with a yawn.

'Put some clothes on and I'll tell you over breakfast.'

'No!' Sug ejaculated adamantly.

'But, Sug …' I tried to reason with him.

'No, Huston. This is not up for discussion. The answer is no.' He made me feel like an unruly child being scolded by its parent.

'Why not?' I asked casually spreading some whip

cream and maple syrup on some waffles.

'Because I am not going to stand by and watch my boyfriend, *my* boyfriend! fuck another guy.'

'But it wouldn't just be me with another guy. It would be you too,' I said.

'Oh, well that makes all the difference,' Sug responded sarcastically.

'I've been doing research on three-ways and from everything I've read people have said that adding a third person or even more …'

'More! For Christ's sake, Huston why don't we just turn the house into a brothel and have orgies every night?'

'Or even more,' I continued as though he hadn't spoken, 'has saved their marriages.'

'We are not teenagers anymore. We are respectable professionals in our 30s. People like us don't do this,' he said, voice rising almost to a shrieking falsetto.

'Actually,' I said, 'older professional couples are more apt to dabble in taboo sex acts and do stuff others would classify as kinky or stuff teenagers would do.' Like all good writers I had done my research.

'The answer is no and we are not going to have any more talk about this. My God, Huston, to think you would even suggest something like this,' he chided, making me feel like the worst person who ever lived. 'Just imagine what would happen if this got out. This is a small town. People talk.'

I wanted to argue with him. God how I wanted to scream and yell and make him see that I was right and he was wrong. What can I say, it's the Texan in me. I wanted to call him old-fashioned. A tyrannical fascist fossil. I had a whole argument planned out in my head about living in the 21st century and about getting with the times. Naturally I won, but the doorbell rang.

'I'll get it,' I said wiping my mouth.

'And no more of this crazy talk, you hear?' Sug said.

'Yes oh, Lord God, King Right,' I answered bowing sarcastically. 'And no more of this crazy talk, you hear?' I mumbled as I made my way towards the door. 'I'll talk about whatever I damn well please. Help you boys?' I asked the two fellows standing on my doorstep.

'We're the contractors,' the older one said.

'Oh. Yeah. The basement. Please come in.' I had completely forgotten they were coming. 'I'm Huston Blake. My daddy has a lot of Texas pride.' I laughed shaking their hands. I said that to everyone I met. It was a bad joke but it was my bad joke.

'Joshua Mallory,' the older gentlemen introduced himself. 'This is my assistant Eduardo Paolo.'

'Duda,' the assistant, who couldn't be a day over 18, said.

'I peg your pardon, honey?' I asked.

'Duda,' he repeated. 'It's my nickname.'

'Cute,' I said, referring to both him and the nickname. 'Well the basement is down those steps. Make yourselves at home. If y'all need anything just holler.'

Duda's gaze lingered on me more than it should have. His dark eyes, twinkling with boyish mischief made me blush with guilt. And we hadn't even done anything but look at each other! Smirking, he followed his boss down the steps. I stood at the top listening to their footsteps grow softer and softer.

'Who was that?' Sug asked coming up behind me and making me jump.

'Contractors. For the basement remodel,' I explained too quickly. My voice was stained with guilt but if he heard it Sug didn't comment.

'I'll be home late,' he said pecking my lips. 'Behave.'

He indicated the basement. I can't believe he actually implied that! Maybe he had heard the unwarranted guilt in my voice after all.

'Don't worry, Sug. You know the only other men in my life are the ones I write about.'

After he was gone I took out a cigarette and puffed away as I stared down into the basement. As much as I tried not to think about Duda I couldn't help it. He was very cute. And young. Barely legal, jail-bait young. I had always heard about young guys and their legendary stamina. Coming several times. Hard-ons for days. Did Duda have all those attributes?

It was several minutes before I realised I was puffing on air. My fingers were blackened. Smokey grey ash littered my feet.

'Easy, Huston,' I whispered.

Walking into the kitchen I took out a fresh cigarette and chain-smoked as I cleaned the breakfast dishes. The kitchen was filled with so much smoke I'm surprised one of the neighbours didn't call the fire department.

'Excuse me,' a young voice behind me made me jump. 'Where is your restroom?'

Turning around, Duda was inches from my face. His scent invaded my nostrils making my penis quiver.

'I hate to ask, but may I use your shower?' he continued. 'It's my parents' anniversary tonight and I'm supposed to meet them at a very fancy restaurant and I'm not sure I'll have time to go home. I have a nice suit in the car but I don't want to meet them looking and smelling like this.' He indicated his body. His skin was stained with paint and there were bits of virginal white plaster in his dark hair. He was so cute. Innocent. Naïve almost. He reminded me of a young Sug. It took all my willpower not to reach out and caress his face.

'Of course, handsome,' I said. 'Help yourself.'

'Thanks.' He smiled wide with gratitude. His smile almost fell off his face. 'I didn't want to say anything in front of my boss, but I'm a big fan of yours. I've read everything you've ever written, including all your short stories.'

'Why thank you darlin',' I returned the smile. 'Shower's upstairs. First on the right.'

I watched him walk up the stairs. His butt fit snugly inside the tight denim. There were a few rips and I made the discovery that Duda didn't wear underwear! Good Lord! It was damn near impossible not to follow him and hop in that shower with him!

Deciding it was safer for me in my office I sat in front of my computer and typed furiously. Believe it or not, it worked. Almost. I almost started to forget all about the hot naked Latin boy in my shower lathering up his hard body. Muscles all wet and soapy. Almost. Until …

'Mr Blake? Mr Blake? Are you still around?'

'In my office, hun. End of the hall,' I called out, not taking my eyes from the screen or missing a keystroke.

'Towels?' He was behind me.

'Linen cabinet. Let me …'

Turning, I lost my breath and found a hard-on. Duda was before me. Little droplets of water made his dark skin glisten. His hair was still damp, water colouring it a dark mocha. His hands were in front of his crotch, barely able to keep himself hidden.

'I'm sorry.' His caramel coloured skin burned beet red. 'I couldn't find any towels.'

'It's all right, hun.' I had trouble getting the words out of my throat that had suddenly been filled to overflowing with cotton. 'I'm a sex writer. You don't have anything I haven't seen before, Sug.'

I froze like a victim of Medusa's. I'd just called him Sug! The only person I ever called Sug was Sug!

I'm fucked, I thought with despair. And not the good kind of fucked.

He turned and that butt! Good Lord that butt. It should be illegal to cover that thing up with pants. Smooth. Muscular. Hard. Crack long and deep.

Down, boy. I closed my eyes and exhaled. Remember the insanely jealous and protective man you got. The man who's a lawyer. The man who probably knows what to do with the evidence. And the body.

Handing him a towel I leaned against the wall and concentrated on trying to get my breathing to return to normal. A force beyond my control pulled my eyes towards the bathroom. The door had been left open a crack.

Dare I?

Oh what harm could it do?

On tiptoes I crept toward the door. The fluffy carpet tickled my toes. I no longer had any control over my movements. I was a marionette being controlled by a puppet master. Reaching the door I took a breath to steady myself and looked in.

I can't believe I'm doing this!

Looking in, I watched Duda turn around and I saw it: long; thick; uncut. He was huge. The biggest I had ever seen. It nearly grazed his knee. And that body: tight; muscular; large dark nipples; hard pecs; large biceps and tree trunks for legs. His whole body was completely devoid of hair except for the shaggy mop on his head.

I stared in shocked amazement at this criminally gorgeous guy walking around my bathroom touching my stuff. Did I mention he was nude?

Duda opened the clothes hamper, took out a pair of my

briefs, brought them to his nose and breathed deeply. His penis grew and he quickly stroked himself to orgasm as he continued smelling my used shorts. I couldn't believe it! Just like something out of one of my books a hot, muscular good looking guy had just stained my tiles with his come. He ran my briefs over his entire body before licking them. I have never been so turned on in my life! Slowly I stroked my hard bulge.

When Duda emerged from the bathroom, fully clothed unfortunately, I was sitting innocently on the bed. We smiled at each other.

'Thank you. Wow! I can't believe I actually showered in Huston Blake's bathroom.'

I can't believe you did some other things in my bathroom, I wanted to say, but instead I merely answered with, 'No problem, handsome.'

He sat down next to me. His hand brushed against mine sending a million tingles through me, causing me to shiver despite the heat wave.

It all happened so fast. Before I knew what was happening our lips were locked together in a fiery embrace. Pushing me onto my back Duda was on top of me, moving his hips back and forth against mine as his hands travelled under my shirt. I was powerless to stop him. I tried. Good Lord I tried. But every time I opened my mouth to ask him to stop it was either invaded by his tongue or moans came out, encouraging him to go on.

Of course it wasn't long before we were naked and Duda's penis was buried balls deep inside my butt. He fucked me rough. Like a whore. We were like animals as he fucked me on the bed I made love with Sug on. Duda had stamina. Lots of it. He was a sex machine, coming inside me three times. Each of his orgasms were more powerful than the last. It was almost like his balls had an unlimited supply of come.

'Wow!' he said afterwards. 'I can't believe I actually fucked Huston Blake. The King Of Gay Erotica. You should write that scene in your next book,' he suggested kissing me tenderly as if we were old lovers.

'Do me a favour.' My voice quivered with shame as I nervously puffed on a cigarette, expecting Sug to come home early. 'Don't tell anyone. This is a small town. People talk.'

'Understood. See you tomorrow.' He kissed me passionately.

Tomorrow! He was coming back to tomorrow to continue remodelling the basement. Quickly I locked the front door, jumped into the shower and scrubbed Duda off my body. I washed the sheets and scrubbed the bathroom clean erasing all traces the boy had ever been there.

Waiting for Sug to come home I smoked a pack of cigarettes in record time and felt like the biggest whore in the world. It wouldn't have been so bad if Duda had been a dud in bed but he was a prize stallion. Just thinking about our fuck session got me hard. I wanted him again and that made me feel like the scum of the earth. I had cheated on Sug – the only man I had ever loved. The only man I had ever been with.

Shit, I thought. Can't say that any more.

With a cigarette dangling between my trembling lips I began to sob. Tomorrow was our anniversary.

Because it was a special occasion Sug called in sick. I was glad. Having him home with me would keep me from doing anything else stupid with Duda. And when he walked in the door with Joshua I was mighty glad Sug was there to save me from my weak willpower. His jeans were so tight I thought they were painted on. It was clear he wore no briefs again today and he did nothing to hide his obscenely large bulge. His jeans were torn, offering peeks of his delicious golden brown flesh. He wore a wife-beater that clung to his muscles, shamelessly displaying him. His nipples were hard as my cock and poked out of the thin fabric.

'Morning, Mr Blake,' he greeted me as if nothing out of the ordinary had happened though his gaze lingered just a little too long.

'Mornin', Joshua. Eduardo. I don't believe you two have met my boyfriend, Nick Mangacavallo.' I made sure to emphasise the boyfriend bit as I glared at Duda.

'Nice to meet you,' Sug said. 'Are you from Mexico?' he asked Duda. 'I detected an accent.'

'Brazil,' Duda answered.

'How long have you been in Texas?' Sug asked while I wished he'd cut the chit-chat shit so the temptation could get out of my sight and maybe my painfully throbbing hard-on would turn limp.

'My family has been here three months. Mr Mallory has been very kind.'

'Well you speak English really well,' Sug complimented. 'Better than most natives.'

'Thank you Mr Mangacavallo.'

'Call me Nick.'

'Nick,' Duda repeated, though his eyes were on me, smiling.

Thankfully Joshua and Duda stayed in the basement. I spent most of the day in my office with Sug having him critique my latest book. Sug was my harshest critic and biggest fan.

At four Joshua and Duda left. Sug told me to go upstairs, get undressed and put on my cowboy hat.

'Let's be spontaneous,' he gleefully exclaimed making me smirk. 'We're going to make love on a Friday night.

Maybe twice. And I'm not wearing the tie. You're getting me completely naked tonight.'

I chuckled and kissed his eager lips. 'You're cute, Sug. And sweet. Don't ever change.'

'Close your eyes,' he called from the hall after I was nude. 'No peeking. You'll spoil the surprise.'

'If you got something pierced I swear to God I'm leaving you.'

He laughed. 'Are your eyes closed?'

'Yes,' I said covering them with my hat.

'You sure?'

'Yes.'

'Promise?'

'Sug, just give me the damn surprise.'

'OK, open 'em. Happy anniversary!' Sug cried out as I regained my sight.

My mouth was opened in stunned wonderment. Sug stood before me completely nude. That's not why I was stunned. Standing on either side of him were Joshua and Duda, also nude and stroking their hard lengths. Their tool belts hung on their hips. It was like something out of a dirty magazine.

Joshua, 20 years older than Sug and I, still had a nice body, kept hard and firm thanks to his work. He was much hairier than Sug. It was a silver-grey colour and gave him a very distinguished dignified look.

'If this is a dream I never want to wake up,' I said causing all three to laugh. 'Sug, what is this?'

'Your present,' he answered, as if I should have known.

'My … present?'

'I did some research online about couples and group sex the other day at the office when I was supposed to be going over Mrs Willowbee's will. Most of the stuff I read was pretty positive. This is my way of saying sorry for being such a close minded jackass.'

Throwing my arms around him, I jumped on him almost knocking him down. I kissed him all over. Soon Joshua and Duda joined us. I don't know when they did it but they had removed their belts. The four of us stood there with roaming hands and passionate lips.

'Suck them in front of me,' Sug whispered, teeth tugging on my earlobe.

He made himself comfortable on the bed, leisurely running his hand up and down his length as I knelt in front of Joshua and Duda. Boss and worker kissed, hands exploring, as I sucked and stroked, making sure to give equal attention to both.

'Swallow them. Together,' Sug gently coached, squeezing his balls.

Unhinging my mouth like a serpent I smiled, savouring the feel of two hard dicks in my mouth. Their pre-come mixed together creating a delectable sexual cocktail. Slowly I sucked, holding onto their full balls. Their hands gripped my hair, holding my head in place as they bucked their hips, fucking my mouth perfectly in sync.

Joining Sug on the bed, he kissed me. Our tongues flicking against each other. Duda went to work on Sug's cock while Joshua fingered my eager hole.

He was gentle with his fingering as he prepared my hole for the sexual feast of cock and come it was about to receive. Inserting first one finger, then a second and even a third, his fingers worked my hole into a frenzy. Like a flower it opened to him inviting his whole fist in! Gasping, I moaned into Sug's mouth. Sug held me in place while Joshua slowly fisted my hole, stretching it to full capacity, until I came.

The orgasm was so intense I nearly passed out. My

eyes rolled back in my head and my heart was beating so rapidly I worried I'd have a heart attack. Tears were actually coming out of my eyes it was that damn good.

Joshua pulled his fist out of me and the four of us licked his fingers clean enjoying the taste of him and I joined as one.

'I want you inside me,' Sug said.

I was shocked. Sug had a virgin hole. The idea of popping his ass cherry turned me on all the more.

Grabbing some lube I lathered up Sug's hole. It puckered when the first cool drops caressed it. Gently I ran my finger in a tiny circle before gently sticking it in. Sug's hole closed around it. Using slow, even strokes I moved my finger in and out.

'Use your tongue, babe,' Sug begged.

As Joshua licked and fingered my own hole my tongue lapped Sug's. His virgin butt was delicious. My tongue flicked against his opening, teasing him. Shoving my tongue deep inside him I stretched his tight little hole. Sug moaned, hips gently bucking.

'Stick it in me, baby,' he groaned, voice a whisper in the wind.

Kneeling behind him, I pushed my penis into his hole. It was so tight. It held me in a vice grip like an anaconda squeezing its prey.

'Son of a bitch!' He moaned. 'That feels so good.'

Laughing I began moving my hips back and forth finding my rhythm. Duda had joined Joshua behind me, both of them fingered me. A contented sigh spilled over my lips when Joshua's plump penis slid inside me. Imagine my surprise when I felt Duda's dick in there too! Talk about a Lucky Pierre! It felt great having two cocks in my ass. It felt even greater taking Sug's ass virginity.

After the four of us had climaxed, Joshua lazily ran

one of his paint brushes over my body. The tiny bristles tickled my skin causing me to tingle all over. He ran the bristles over my hole before whispering:

'Lay on your back.'

I did. He spread my legs and inserted the paintbrush inside me. The bristles hit every erogenous zone I had. My stomach quivered and I felt my eyes roll back in my head a second time as the three took turns fucking me with the brush.

'I want to do something,' Duda said picking up a long wooden paint stirrer. 'I saw this in a porno once. Get on your hands and knees.

I did as I was told. Duda slapped my face with the stick. Once. Twice. Three Times. Each time the impact had a little bit more force. Moving down he slapped my chest, penis and balls. I moaned with each slap. I enjoyed it more than I thought I would. He slapped my ass with the hard wooden stick, making my cheeks jiggle. He slapped my ass harder and harder. The loud thwacks bounced off the walls.

Joshua and Sug were kissing, fingers getting lost in the other's chest hair. Their cocks, hard as granite, were pressed up against each other.

Duda spread my cheeks and inserted the long stirrer. I was on my hands and knees, rock hard, with a hard wooden tail anxiously wondering what Duda had in mind. I smiled with anticipation. The only time I ever got this kinky was in my books. It felt great to finally unleash my inner whore.

Glancing over my shoulder I watched the other end of the stirrer disappear inside him. Our cheeks touched and we rocked back and forth. Our balls slapped against each other. I had never felt such pleasure in my life.

'Now that's a beautiful sight,' Sug whistled

approvingly. 'Those porno people had the right idea.'

Adjusting my crooked hat, Sug kissed me full on the lips. Joshua and Duda's lips were locked as Joshua vigorously jerked his employee off.

Soon Sug found himself underneath me. Joshua was underneath Sug who was lying flat as a board on Joshua as he pumped in and out of Sug's hole. I was riding Sug like a buckin' fuckin' bronco.

'Oh yeah,' Sug moaned. 'You have a great ass,' he grunted slapping it. 'Ride my cock, cowboy!'

Grinding against his hardness I clutched the cowboy hat and let out a hardy yeehaw!

Duda's head was buried in my lap, greedily feasting on my length. Pulling the young boy up I kissed him enjoying my taste on his full lips.

'Hop on, handsome,' I said with a wink.

Duda impaled himself on my penis. I gripped his meaty thickness in my fist. Our four moans became one. The bedsprings squealed out the rhythm of our fucking. We came as one, crying out at the intensity of the orgasm.

'Happy anniversary,' Sug said, kissing me.

'Happy anniversary, Sug. I love you.'

'I love you, Huston.'

After Duda and Joshua had cleaned up and left, Sug came into the bedroom with some paint and a huge grin on his face. We painted each other's bodies ridiculous colours. I even drew a happy face with a huge purple polka-dotted Afro on his butt. Getting some ties he bound my hands and feet and tied one around my neck like a bridal. He took out one of my cigarettes, ran it temptingly between my lips – good Lord I wanted it so bad! – before sticking it in my hole.

'Light it,' he said after he had fucked me with it.

I did, enjoying the mixture of tobacco and my hole.

Who knew a four-way was all it took to unleash Sug's inner horny man. Taking my cigarette Sug took a puff and blew the smoke into my hole before burying first his face in there and then his hard-on. We made love for hours. Sug kept tight hold of the tie around my neck and he kept moaning my name …

'Huston,' Sug's voice brought me back to reality. 'Come to bed. It's late. Plus it's Wednesday. You know what Wednesday means. Hump day!'

I looked at the fantasy I had written. My deepest fantasy that I so wanted to come true. I looked at Sug, nude except for the tie that hung loosely around his neck.

'New story?' he asked. 'May I?'

'Always, Sug.'

I got up and Sug made himself comfortable. Placing my arms around him I kissed his neck and stroked his dark chest hair, wondering if life would ever imitate fiction ….

Slash rode goofy past the *No Skateboarding on Sidewalk* sign because he always rode on the sidewalk and he looked in the store windows as he passed.

I rode through the shopping centre parking lot, matching his speed but about five feet back. He darted among slow-moving shoppers still dressed in their church clothes and I dodged minivans and SUVs driven by soccer moms who paid more attention to the rug rats inside than the traffic outside their vehicles.

He wore baggy blue-jean board shorts, a tight-fitting black wife-beater that revealed the tat sleeves inked from his shoulders to his wrists, and he had his finger-length black hair spiked. I wasn't nearly so brave, nor so fashionable. My blond hair hadn't been combed in days, and I wore jeans, a long-sleeved black hoodie, and thin black leather gloves. I was nowhere near as good as Slash, and I'd slammed so many times I think the palms of my hands will for ever have the texture of coarse-grain sandpaper. That's why I'd started wearing the gloves.

As Slash approached the end of the shopping mall's sidewalk, the old lady who owned the Sew-n-Sew at the south end of the mall stepped out of her store and yelled at him.

'Can't you read? How many times do I have to chase

you hoodlums down? I'm going to call the police!'

She never did.

Slash smiled at her and did an acid drop off the curb at the end of the sidewalk. I kicked a little harder and caught up to him.

'Why do you torment her like that?' I yelled.

'Why does *she* torment *me*?' Slash yelled back. 'Skateboarding's not a crime!'

We'd spent the morning at the skatepark with Tall Tony and some of the other guys and were on our way to my garage apartment, where I had an unopened box of frosted strawberry Pop-Tarts on the kitchen counter and two quarts of Mountain Dew in the refrigerator. It wasn't much, but it was more than Slash had offered me for dinner at his place two days earlier.

Slash and I had met at the skatepark and we'd been together almost two years. I was taking accounting classes at the junior college, lived over my grandparents' garage, and relied on my parents for most of my pocket money, something they would only dole out if I maintained a B average. Slash, barely a year older than me, worked part-time at a bike shop and spent most of his available time at the skatepark perfecting his technique.

His uncle gave Slash his first skateboard, and as soon as he could nail some basic tricks Slash started entering contests. He wanted to turn pro, but he hadn't been able to attract the attention of sponsors. They didn't even comp him boards or other cool stuff. It wasn't about boarding ability, they told him, it's about attitude and marketability, and they didn't see anything in Slash that they didn't see in dozens of other boarders. Their attitude frustrated Slash because he didn't know how to make himself stand out from the pack.

I kept telling him that his time would come. Maybe

that's why he hung with me even though I pretty much suck as a skateboarder. I might have been the only person in his life who believed in him.

We pounded up the stairs, parked our boards on the couch, and stepped into my kitchen, which was nothing more than the other half of my living room, with a counter, sink, fridge, and stove along the wall opposite the couch. Slash tore open the Pop-Tarts box while I retrieved the two bottles of Mountain Dew from the fridge. He handed me one of the foil-wrapped packs of Pop-Tarts and I handed him one of the two-litre bottles of Dew.

My apartment had only two rooms – the living room/kitchen and the bedroom – with a three-quarter bath accessible through the bedroom. I had decorated by taping posters of Tony Hawk and pictures of other boarders torn out of the skateboarding magazines to the living room walls. Some were pictures of famous skaters, and others were pictures of guys doing rad tricks. The bedroom contained a double bed and a desk where I did my homework, had more posters taped to the walls, and had a pile of dirty laundry in one corner because I was too lazy to carry everything downstairs for my grandmother to wash.

After we ate, Slash led me into the bedroom. He didn't have to say anything; I knew what he wanted. He wanted what he always wanted after a morning of boarding. He wanted me to go down on him.

When I unfastened Slash's belt, his oversized board shorts dropped off his slim hips and hit the floor, pooling around his ankles. He didn't wear anything beneath the shorts except the snake tattooed on his lower abdomen, and his thick cock already stood erect.

I still wore my gloves and I wiped my palms on my pants to rid them of dirt from my frequent slams. Then I dropped to my knees, wrapped one gloved fist around Slash's turgid cock, and began pistoning my fist up and down. As I jerked off my skateboarding partner, I leaned forward and took the head of his cock in my mouth, hooked my teeth behind his glans, and painted his cockhead with my saliva.

Then, while still pumping my leather-clad hand up and down Slash's fat phallus, I leaned forward, slowing taking in half his length before drawing back. His cock meat tasted salty and sweaty and I licked the underside of his shaft as I moved forward and back. I did the same thing twice more before I reached around Slash, grabbed the firm cheeks of his ass, and pulled his crotch tight against my face, accepting his entire length into my oral cavity for the first time. Slash's heavy ball sack pressed against my chin and his dark, curly hair tickled my nose. I sucked and sucked hard.

My cock grew rigid in my jeans, but I couldn't do anything about it right then. I was concentrating on pleasing my skateboarding partner.

Slash's slim hips began to move as he drew his cock back. Then he pushed forward and drew back, his ass muscles tightening in my hands as he pushed forward. He grabbed the back of my head, wrapping his fingers in my hair, and fucked my face hard and fast, his heavy ball sack slapping against my chin with every thrust. Then Slash's cock exploded and he shot wad after wad of hot come against the back of my throat.

I eagerly swallowed every drop of Slash's come before licking his cock clean. When I finished, Slash stepped backward. His flaccid cock dropped from my mouth and slapped against his thigh.

He stepped out of the blue-jean board shorts, pooled at his ankles and dropped backward on my bed. I admired his slim, muscular body for a moment, but something else demanded my attention. I had an erection, and it was tangled in my boxers. I reached into my pants to untangle my cock before standing. Then I stepped into the bathroom, dropped my pants, and settled onto the toilet seat. After I removed my gloves, I took my cock in my fist and quickly polished my knob.

Then I joined Slash on the bed and we talked about nothing in particular.

Later, we headed back to the skatepark so that Slash could spend Sunday evening practicing, and we returned by backtracking along the same route that had taken us from the park to my garage apartment. I was half a block behind Slash as we approached the shopping mall because I had face-planted two blocks earlier, and I was trying hard to catch up. Many of the stores had already closed for the evening, leaving only the Dollar General open and the Sew-n-Sew turning out its lights as we approached.

Slash walled the curb and continued onto the sidewalk. As he passed the front door of the Sew-n-Sew, several things seemed to happen at once.

A minivan with a soccer mom at the wheel and a prepubescent girl playing with a cell phone in the front passenger seat nosed into a parking space in front of the Sew-n-Sew, the minivan's headlights illuminating the front of the darkened store.

The old lady who owned the place, a bulky purse slung on one arm and heavy key ring in her free hand, stepped out of her shop and turned to lock the door.

A big guy in dark clothing ran around the end of the building, grabbed the old lady's purse, and ran away from me, going the same direction as Slash and gaining ground on him.

I yelled.

The old lady yelled.

The woman and the girl in the minivan yelled.

Slash glanced over his shoulder, saw what was happening, and did something I'd never seen him or any other skateboarder do. He stomped on his board's kickback as he dismounted, flipping his board into the air. He landed flatfoot on the sidewalk, grabbed his board out of the air with both hands and, holding it straight out in front of him with the deck perpendicular to the ground, spun almost 90 degrees and slammed the deck into the purse-snatcher's face, smashing the bigger man's nose and knocking him smooth out.

I reached the two of them at the same time the old lady did. She jerked her purse out of the unconscious man's hand and cursed him with that antiquated language she used when she yelled at Slash for skateboarding on the sidewalk.

'You going to call the police?' I asked.

'I'll call them,' said the soccer mom, who had hurried to where we stood and already had her cell phone out. Her daughter walked behind her, holding her cell phone in front of her as if she was capturing everything with the video function.

I checked the purse-snatcher to ensure that he was breathing, but I didn't do anything about the blood pouring from his nose. I was more concerned with Slash's board, and he assured me that it was fine. Then three of us stood over the unconscious purse-snatcher while the girl started talking on her cell phone and Slash paced back and forth.

Two patrol cars arrived a few minutes later with lights flashing and sirens blaring. Two burly cops with more attitude than brains saw the bleeding scratches on my forehead from my face plant earlier that evening, and they rushed toward Slash before the old lady caught their attention and directed them toward the purse-snatcher, who was conscious but still laying flat on his back.

One cop called an ambulance and stood guard over the purse-snatcher while the other took statements from each of us. The old lady – Mrs Winston – had the Sew-n-Sew's weekend receipts in her purse and was planning to drop them in her bank's night deposit on her way home, so she was grateful that her purse had not been successfully snatched. After the police left, she thanked Slash and then reopened the Sew-n-Sew so the soccer mom could purchase fabric to make something her daughter needed at school Monday morning. Slash and I sat on the curb until the soccer mom and her daughter finally left and Mrs Winston was safely in her car and headed toward the bank.

Slash was amped up when we returned to my apartment. As soon as we had the door closed behind us and had dumped our boards on my couch, he pulled me into his arms and planted his lips on mine. Then he buried his tongue in my mouth.

His kiss was deep, hard, and aggressive. He practically tore my clothes off as we moved to the bedroom, and by the time we were naked we both had erections. I grabbed a half-used tube of lube from my desk, squeezed a dollop onto my palm, and wrapped my hand around Slash's cock. I pumped up and down a couple of time to ensure that his shaft was completed covered. Then I wiped away the glistening drop of pre-come from the tip of his cock and covered his cockhead with lube.

He spun me around and I climbed onto the bed, kneeling on the edge for a moment before dropping to all fours. Slash stepped between my legs, grabbed my hips, and pulled my ass toward him as he thrust his cock into my ass crack. The lube-slick head of his cock pressed against my sphincter and then, with one firm thrust, he buried his cock deep inside me.

Slash drew back and then plunged forward again, his strong fingers gripping my hips so tight I was afraid I might be left with bruises. He fucked me hard and fast, and when he came, he came hard. He slammed into me one last time and then held my ass tight against his groin while he filled me with his come.

Then he did something he didn't usually do. While still holding my hip with one hand, he reached around with the other and grabbed my turgid cock. I braced myself on one hand like a tripod and covered his fist with my free hand. I was so turned on by Slash's aggression and sudden interest in my satisfaction that I came quickly, spewing come over our hands.

When my cock stopped spasming, I pulled away from Slash and rolled onto my back. I still held his hand, so I pulled it to my mouth, wrapped my lips around his fingers, and licked them clean.

By the time I finished licking his fingers, Slash had another erection.

We fucked twice more that night before we finished off the Pop-Tarts and the Mountain Dew and fell asleep watching some really gay horror movie.

Slash went to the skatepark the next morning and I went to class at the junior college. I was sitting in the middle of the quad, a copy of one of the Norton Anthologies open in my lap and my skateboard on the bench next to me, when Tall Tony, a journalism major who boarded with us, did a wheel-slide and came to a halt in front of me.

'Dude,' he said as he stepped off his board, 'did you

see Slash's video on YouTube?'

I looked up. Tony stands well over six feet tall and he's thin as a rail. 'What video?'

'The one where he jumps off his board and smashes a guy in the face,' he said.

'When did you see that?'

'This morning. I was killing time before class when I saw it.' He dropped onto the bench next to me, opened his backpack, and pulled out his Apple laptop. 'Let me show you.'

Tony booted up his computer and logged onto the junior college's wireless network. He had bookmarked a video labelled, *Skateboarder knocks out purse-snatcher,* and a moment later I watched a replay of the previous evening.

I'd been right: the prepubescent girl in the minivan had been recording everything with her cell phone's camera, but someone had edited the video so that it started with the purse snatching and ended with the snatcher laying flat on his back. The girl had gotten excellent footage of Slash kicking his board up, catching it, and swinging it, so that I could see exactly what he did even though I knew I would never be able to duplicate the move.

'Did you see what he did?' Tony asked. 'It was awesome.'

'I know,' I told him. 'I was there.'

He seemed surprised. 'So what really happened?'

I told him everything.

When I finished, Tony pulled an iPhone out of his camouflage shorts pocket, dialled, and pressed the phone to his ear. 'Yo, Dad, you need to hear this.'

Then he repeated everything I'd just told him about the previous evening and added, 'I'll email you his cell phone number and the link to the video.'

197

After Tony finished his call and email, he said, 'My dad's a producer for *Channel 5 News*.'

The next few days were wicked crazy. By the time I finished my last class of the day, a reporter from *Channel 5 News* had interviewed Slash down at the skatepark and Mrs Winston at the Sew-n-Sew.

That night I watched the story of the "Skateboard Hero" with Slash sitting next to me on my couch. The report included the girl's video of the event, Mrs Winston being effusive about what a hero Slash turned out to be, and Slash telling the reporter that he hadn't done anything special. 'I just did what anybody would do.'

Within 24 hours the story of the Skateboard Hero was all over the network news, the cable news networks, and the Internet.

Slash finally stood out from the crowd. By the end of the week he had a sponsor and had a new trick named after him: The Slash-n-Burn.

Slash's 15 minutes of fame as the Skateboard Hero didn't last long. The news cycle passed him by, but by then he was living his dream, earning a living as a pro skateboarder, first by demonstrating his move at various events and then by participating in and sometimes winning competitions.

I stayed in school, studied accounting, and helped Slash manage his money as his income grew. By the time I graduated from a four-year university, Slash had several endorsement deals – including a non-paying one for the Sew-n-Sew after Mrs Winston made the mall's owners take down the *No Skateboarding on Sidewalk* sign – that I helped him negotiate, and we had moved into an old Victorian that I was renovating while he travelled.

I'd been right. I'd told Slash his time would come if he

did the right thing.
He had.
And it had.

The Collaring
by Penelope Friday

He kneels, naked, in the middle of the floor, watching as I get dressed. He may not move until I say he can. I have given permission for him to look at me, though he is forbidden to get hard, no matter what I say or do.

I am choosing my costume for tonight.

Later, I will choose one for Matt, my sub. I am taking him out tonight. I pull a pair of trousers out of the wardrobe, consider them, and reject them. I want everything to be right, tonight. I want it to be perfect. The tight leather trousers I find next are precisely what I want.

I hear Matt moaning as I pull them over my body. They meld to my crotch, leaving little to the imagination. I look down at my submissive. His cock is leaving little to the imagination, either.

'Matt ...' I say warningly.

He bows his head. 'Sorry, Master.'

'Today, of all days, to disobey me.' I am kind, but disapproving. I run my hand over his face and neck, tugging at the collar which is his only clothing. 'Do you want me to remove this?'

'No. Please.'

His erection has subsided at the threat. The familiar pleasure of willingly submitted power is keeping me hard, however. His eyes flicker to my groin, then away, quickly. I see him clench his fingers, digging his nails into his palms in an attempt to control his body's urges.

'Good boy.'

I pull a shirt on, then my thick leather boots, and then look down at Matt. I will be wearing the leather; I will dress my sub in simple denim. The only leather he will wear will be the collar. I smile at him, and run my fingers round his neck, following the collar's path. Then I give him his clothes, and he dresses. I look at my watch.

'Time we were going, Matt.'

'May I stand?'

I nod. 'Walk a pace behind me. You know your place.'

'Yes, Master.'

When we arrive at the hall, our guests have already arrived. Matt keeps a pace behind me, and seems as if he wishes to be entirely hidden; but he trusts me to take care of him, to take care of his needs. This is what it is all about.

'It's all right, Matt,' I murmur soothingly, stroking his arm gently. To my surprise, he is actually trembling.

The room has silenced as they notice our presence. Jerome has taken it upon himself to organise things, and he directs people to seats on either side of the room. Then, with a mocking smile at me, he jerks his head forward.

'Your show now, Kris,' he says.

Followed by Matt, I walk to the front of the room, and turn to address the audience. Matt kneels down by my side, facing me, his eyes lowered. He is shaking again, although it will not be noticeable to anyone except me. I speak.

'As you all know, Matt and I have been in a happy relationship for more than a year,' I say. 'Today, we choose to make a public commitment to each other. I have asked you here to witness our commitment and to see us make our vows.'

Our friends are cheering, but Jerome continues his good work, and silences them quickly. I look down at Matt.

'Matthew?' I say quietly.

He gulps, and rests one hand against my leg for a second, as if seeking support. But when he speaks, his voice is loud and clear.

'I, with open heart and mind, do request Kris, my Master, to take control of my mind and body. I humbly ask him to accept me as his slave, and to use my body as he wishes in order for our relationship to grow and thrive.' Matt's voice chokes on the final words. I reach down and squeeze his hand gently.

'I, with open heart and mind, accept your submission to me, and promise to do all I can to foster our relationship in happiness and health.' I look down at my love, my slave, my possession. 'As a sign of this agreement, I give to you this silver collar as an outward sign of my Mastership.'

I give Matt my hand and encourage him to his feet, unfasten the leather collar, and replace it with the silver collar, which I padlock shut, placing the key on a chain around my own neck. 'The collar represents your agreement; the key represents mine.'

Our friends, the few chosen guests, cheer as I kiss my submissive and claim him.

'Thank you, Master,' Matt whispers.

'And you are mine, now and for always?'

'Yes, Master.'

I smile. There is one last step to be taken to conclude our vows. 'Prove it,' I demand.

Matt looks at me, and then at the group of people who have come to see our official collaring.

'Now?'

In answer, I push him to the floor, unbuckling my trousers to allow my cock to spring free.

'You know what to do.'

Matt lifts his head, and takes my cock into his mouth. He is hesitant; shyer than usual. He is not used to an audience. As I look down on him, I see the back of his neck is burning bright red around the new, silver, collar. I twist my fingers in his hair in encouragement, forcing him to take me in deeper, deeper.

He is nearly choking as I hit the back of his throat, and I can see that he is embarrassed by the enthusiasm displayed by our friends. But at the same time, he cannot help but enjoy what he is doing; his own cock is leaping to attention. I thrust a booted foot between his legs to rub against his erection, and I can feel the hissed breath he takes around my cock.

I have known him long enough to know what turns him on; and the smell of the leather, and of sex, has ever stirred his desire. I am struggling to hold on to my composure as he bobs in front of me, swirling his practised tongue around my erection. His mouth is hotter than ever, despite the audience – or maybe, because of it. Who knows? Perhaps Matt has discovered his inner exhibitionist. I suspect that I do not care as long as he keeps doing what he's doing now.

But I do not want to come here, like this. Difficult though it is to do, I pull away.

'Good boy,' I say approvingly, as he looks hopefully at me. I know what he is thinking, and this is his day, his and mine. 'Yes, Matt,' I nod.

I reach down and unbutton his jeans, pushing them around his knees. He turns around for me, giving me a perfect view of his almost perfect arse.

Jerome, wolf-whistling, throws me a tube of lubrication, and I smooth it over Matt's hole, pressing first one, then two, then three fingers inside him. Finally, I kneel behind him, pushing my knob into him with gentle slowness. He loves me to be slow at first, but as I continue to move with teasing unhurried strokes, he groans. I know he wants to push back against me, to hump his hips and let me fuck him hard, but he is forbidden to move unless I allow it. I reach my hand (still slippery with lube) around him to grasp his cock and slide up and down with the same frustrating deliberateness, until neither of us can bear it any longer.

Our guests are forgotten in our meeting of bodies; and I allow him to move now.

'Come on, Matt, that's right,' I whisper in his ear. 'Fuck yourself on me.'

And he is panting and humping and thrusting back against me, as my fingers work faster on his cock. And he cries, 'Please, Master!' as I feel my own orgasm coming close. I come, in a medley of light and blackness, groaning my release. As my fingers touch Matt's collar, he knows he is allowed the same response and his come is spurting through my fingers, as he covers the floor with his spunk.

The audience is applauding, and I twist my submissive round to give him a kiss.

'Yours,' he mutters hotly.

'Mine,' I agree.

Matt, my love, my slave, my submissive. Now and for ever.